The Bl...

Other books by Laura Leone:

Romance Novels:
> One Sultry Summer
> A Wilder Name
> Ulterior Motives
> Guilty Secrets
> A Woman's Work
> Upon a Midnight Clear
> Celestial Bodies
> The Bandit King
> The Black Sheep
> Sleight of Hand
> Untouched by Man
> Under the Voodoo Moon
> Fever Dreams

Written as Laura Resnick:

Fantasy Novels:
> In Legend Born
> In Fire Forged

Non-Fiction
> A Blond in Africa

The Black Sheep
Laura Leone

WILDSIDE PRESS
Berkeley Heights, New Jersey

First Wildside Press edition: October 2000

Author's Note

All the characters in this book have no existence outside the imagination of the author and have no relation whatsoever to anyone
bearing the same name or names. They are not even distantly inspired by any individual known or unknown to the author, and all
incidents are pure invention.

The Black Sheep
A publication of
Wildside Press
P.O. Box 45
Gillette, NJ 07933-0045
www.wildsidepress.com

SECOND EDITION

For my friend Erma Jean,
with thanks for holding my hand again

All thy vexations
Were but trials of thy love, and thou
Hast strangely stood the test: here, afore Heaven,
I ratify this my rich gift.
— William Shakespeare
The Tempest

One

He sprawled naked across the vast bed, abandoning himself to the unaccustomed luxury of clean cotton sheets, plump goose down pillows, and a firm, springy mattress. Years of sleeping in pup tents and on the hard ground had made him appreciative of such simple pleasures.

The scent of lemon groves and the sound of the sea drifted through the balcony doors of the bedroom. The shadows shifted as the sun rose higher, and he gradually felt its warm rays slanting through the windows and fanning across his face, urging him to rise up and seize the day.

His black lashes fluttered as he considered opening his eyes. He hadn't really been asleep, the sweet oblivion of sleep still eluding him for the most part. Instead, he floated in a vague fog of semi-consciousness, too restless to sleep, too exhausted to fully awaken.

Drowsily, he pondered his options. He could get up and call the clinic — assuming the phones worked today; he could get up and close the shutters; or he could just roll over.

He sighed and rolled over. He kicked away the sheet and soaked up the soothing heat of the Mediterranean sunshine as it spilled across the bed. The bedroom windows faced north, so the intrusion of the sun meant it must be around noon. He sighed again, opened his eyes, and stared at the ornately carved baroque dresser occupying the far wall.

Around noon. Maybe he should get up.

He was usually an early riser, up and active by dawn. But that was before he'd awoken one morning halfway around the world from here to find his little sister hovering in the void between life and death. That was before she'd clawed her nails down his cheek when he told her he'd made arrangements for her to go to a treatment center.

He rolled over on his back and stared at the ceiling, feeling all the pain welling up inside him again, hot and raw. *Lisa, forgive me. It's what someone should have done for my mother, it's what I had to do for you.*

Anger pulsed inside him, too. Damn their father, damn Lisa's own mother! Why was it left up to *him* to take charge again?

He threw a darkly tanned forearm across his eyes, willing the hurt to go away, but knowing it wouldn't. He swallowed back his bitterness with effort. After all, why should things be any different this time?

It never changed. He had seen it his whole life. His mother, his father, his stepmother, Lisa, and the people around them had all paid an insanely high price for the dubious benefits of fame. He must have been crazy to have considered, however tentatively, going back to the States for good this time.

He had gone through hell in Los Angeles, waiting for the verdict on his sister's life, then making his own verdict on her future. And so, needing to heal, needing to curl up and lick his wounds in private, he had come here, to his mother's house on this quiet, sun-drenched Mediterranean island. The only serenity he could remember from his tumultuous childhood was wrapped up in this house, these vineyards, these olive and lemon groves. He had always been happy here, and even after his mother's death, it had continued to be a place of healing and contentment for him, a place he could come to replenish his strength.

The phone rang shrilly, making his body jerk in surprise.

"Glory be, the phones work," he muttered. Now who could be calling? Anyone on the island who wanted to talk to him would simply knock on his door.

Lisa. With fear clutching at his belly, he reached for the receiver. "Hello?" He blinked, remembering he was in Italy, and amended, *"Pronto?"* His voice sounded thick and fuzzy.

"Don't tell me I woke you!" came his brother's voice, crackling and muffled, all the way from New York. "It must be past noon there!"

He rubbed his eyes and said blandly, "Hi, Vince." He glanced at the clock on the nightstand. "Yeah, just past noon."

"You don't sound so good, Roe." There was a slight pause, then Vince continued in a different tone. "I heard about your sister. I'm so sorry. How's she doing?"

Ten years older than Roe's thirty-four, Vince had been born to the same mother, though he was from her first marriage and Roe from her second. A dozen years younger than Roe, Lisa was the daughter of Roe's father, from his second marriage. Though Roe maintained sporadic contact with both his siblings, Vince and Lisa had only met a couple of times over the years.

"How's she doing?" Roe repeated. "Just great. She nearly killed herself with a combination of alcohol and cocaine, and now she's in a treatment center, hating me and swearing she'll never forgive me for this. I think that about covers it."

"You did what was best," Vince said, clearly meaning it.

"God knows my father wouldn't have had the guts to do it, even if he'd taken a few days off from his show in Vegas to come see her in the hospital in LA."

"He didn't even go to see her?"

"No. Sent his regrets and a few dozen roses." Roe's voice was desert dry. "And as for Candy . . ." Roe rolled his eyes as he referred to Lisa's mother, actress Candice Jirrell. "We'd probably all have been better off if Candy *hadn't* turned up. When I left, she was busy telling half of Hollywood how I had forced her to send her baby to some clinic."

"*Did* you force her?"

Roe shifted on the bed. "Yeah, I guess so."

"I'm glad you took charge, Roe. I've seen this coming for years."

Roe grimaced and closed his eyes. "No wonder I never go home," he mumbled. His first trip to Los Angeles in three years had been intended as a vacation, a chance to visit with his sister while he decided whether or not he wanted to move back to the States. Within days it had turned into his worst nightmare, a reprise of his mother's death, and he had barely stopped it in time.

"You *are* home," Vince reminded him.

"Yeah," Roe said after a moment. "You're right. Sontara is home." He frowned. "How'd you know I was here?" He'd flown from Nairobi to LA nearly two weeks earlier. Lisa overdosed within three days of his arrival, before he'd even called Vince to let him know he was in the States. He had spent several more days at the hospital, making difficult decisions. After that, he had spent a full day at the clinic, stoically bearing his sister's venom, then flown out again. Pausing only long enough to change planes, he'd caught a flight from New York to Palermo, the capital city of Sicily, then finally taken the ferry from Trápani to Sontara. "I didn't tell anyone except the administrators at the clinic where I was going."

"I didn't know," Vince admitted. "I called Zu Aspanu, and he told me you were there on the island."

Roe pulled himself up to a sitting position, wondering why Vince had called their uncle. They both knew the old man hated telephones and had only had one installed because their mother, his adored sister, had insisted on it years ago. And phone service on Sontara was so unreliable anyhow that all but the most important messages were sent by letter. "You called Zu Aspanu this morning?" he asked uneasily.

"Yes."

"And now you're calling me. Is it bad news?"

"No, no, of course not." Vince hesitated. "Not really." He drew a breath. "Not necessarily."

"Go on." They might go years without seeing each other, and they might come from a bizarrely disjointed family, but their Sicilian mother had instilled certain values in them that they could never forget. Vince was his brother, and if he had some kind of problem, Roe would do anything in the world to help him.

"It's that gastritis I was having last year," Vince began. "Now don't get crazy on me, but it turns out it's not gastritis after all."

"It's your heart?" Roe guessed quickly.

"Yes. I've already made one trip to the emergency room, and considering my heredity . . . Well, the doctors want to do some surgery. I don't want you to worry, though."

"Vince!" Roe blinked rapidly and came to his knees. He had never even seen Vince's father, their mother's first husband, who had died in his mid-forties of a massive coronary. Vince himself, in Roe's opinion, was a walking time bomb even without hereditary considerations — a tense, nervous, high-strung, competitive, middle-aged, chainsmoking, overweight perfectionist who never exercised or relaxed.

"It's all right," Vince insisted. "The surgery has a high success rate, according to my doctor."

"How long will you be in the hospital?" Roe demanded.

"About a week. Then I'll be recovering at home for about a month."

"Do you want me to come to New York?"

"No, it's okay, Roe. Alice and Michael will both be here," Vince assured him, referring to his wife and teenage son. "And I've got everything under control."

Yes, Roe thought wryly, Vince would definitely have everything under control. Controlling things was Vince's mission in life, a legacy of their tempestuous childhood as Adelina Marino's sons.

They continued to talk about Vince's impending surgery, Roe pressing him for exact dates and detailed information about the procedure. Influenced by Vince's repeated assurance that the doctors predicted a successful operation, Roe finally felt the tension between his shoulders begin to ease a little.

"I'm glad you called to tell me, Vince," he said at last.

"Actually, Roe," Vince began hesitantly, "that's not exactly why I called. I didn't even tell Zu Aspanu about this, and I'd rather you didn't. He'd get all panicky and start laying votive offerings on the shrine at Santa Cecilia."

Roe grinned, knowing the description was accurate. "Okay, I'll keep quiet. So why *did* you call?"

"I need a favor."

"Sure."

"Well, you may not like it when you hear it. I . . . I didn't know you'd be staying there right now."

"Oh?"

"It's about Gingie."

Roe knew that Gingie was the rock star whose career Vince had been managing since shortly after their mother's death some ten years earlier.

Although he had never met Gingie, Roe knew enough about her reputation to suspect Vince was right — he wasn't going to like this request. "What about her?"

"I need to put her somewhere while I'm laid up," Vince said matter-of-factly.

"You need to put her somewhere?" Roe repeated. "You make it sound like you're kenneling a dog."

"Perhaps I chose my words poorly," Vince admitted. "How can I put it? Two weeks ago, I genuinely hoped it would be enough to simply ask Gingie to stay out of trouble while I was convalescing."

"So ask her," Roe said.

"I can't. I've come to my senses. It's impossible."

"Come on, Vince. She's an adult. She ought to be able to keep a low profile for a month or so."

"Oh, Roe," Vince said wearily. "The thought of Gingie running amok in New York for a whole month, with no restraints, no guidance, no one to control her impulses . . . It makes my chest hurt."

"Don't think about it, then," Roe said quickly, wondering what kind of virago Gingie must be. "So send her home to her family or something."

"No, I can't. You don't know her family. Anyhow, recent events have proven beyond a shadow of a doubt that I need to get her far, far away from here, someplace so remote that no one will ever find her. Only then will I rest easy."

"Recent events?" Roe frowned and ran a hand through his wavy black hair, trying to bring an elusive memory into focus. "I read . . . something about her. Some kind of scandal?"

"I didn't know you read the tabloids," Vince chided.

"I read everything lying on the coffee table in the waiting room at the hospital last week." Roe tried to remember what he had read about Gingie. At the time, he had been too preoccupied to pay much attention to the antics of one blond rock star, a woman so successful that she was the only client Vince managed anymore. A woman so troublesome, if Roe recalled Vince's tales of woe accurately, that she was also the only client that even a workaholic like Vince had time or strength to manage.

"Well, if you read about what happened, I'm sure you'll agree that I need to get her out of here until things cool off."

Roe went absolutely still. "You want to send her to Sontara?"

"It's perfect," Vince insisted eagerly. "Quiet, remote, isolated. There are probably only a dozen telephones on the whole island, and *no* journalists, television cameras, or photographers. I thought I'd put her in the villa, have Zu Aspanu hire a cook and a maid for her from the village. . . ."

"Well, think of another plan, Vince. *I'm* here, and I'm not sharing

the house with some scandal-scented rock singer." Although he and
Vince co-owned the villa, having jointly inherited it from their mother,
it had always been Roe's refuge rather than Vince's. He resented the
intrusion.

"It doesn't have to be for a whole month. We could compromise,"
Vince offered.

"I don't want to compromise," Roe said stubbornly. "I've got a sister
who's just nearly died and may never speak to me again. Now I've got
a brother going into the hospital for heart surgery. I came to Sontara
to clear my head, and I don't want someone hanging around here being
shrill and demanding."

"*I'm* the brother who's going into the hospital for heart surgery,"
Vince reminded him, "and Gingie is not shrill and demanding. She's
just . . . a little unique in her approach to life."

"No, Vince."

"I'll make the rules very clear to her before I put her on the plane."

"Don't do this to me, Vince."

"I can't think of any other place she's likely to stay out of trouble.
And I'll sleep so much better knowing she's with you.

"It's out of the question."

"You'll keep an eye on her . . ."

"It's not even open to debate."

"You'll make sure no one knows she's there . . ."

"Vince, are you listening to me?"

"Come on, Roe, have I ever asked you for anything?"

"Now that I think about it," Roe said through gritted teeth, "you ask
for something totally unreasonable every single time I talk to you."

"And how often is that?" Vince demanded, easily changing the
subject. "Do xou ever call me from Zimbabwe or Rwanda or Morocco,
or wherever the hell you go traipsing around year after year?"

"Not this again, Vince, please," Roe sighed. "Sometimes you sound
like Mom."

There was a long pause before Vince said, "It would mean a lot to
me, Roe. You'd be taking a tremendous load off my mind."

"I don't want your 'tremendous load' on Sontara," he protested, but
he could feel himself weakening.

"She'll be as quiet as a mouse," Vince promised, obviously lying
through his teeth.

"Can't you find someplace else to stow your keg of dynamite?" Roe
pleaded, sensing he had lost the argument.

"Oh, my chest . . ." Vince moaned.

"Okay, I'll take her," Roe ground out, vulnerable to his brother's
unforgivably obvious ploy. "But the *second* you're feeling better, I'm
shipping her back to you. Got that?"

"Absolutely." Vince could afford to be magnanimous now.

"And I don't want her disrupting my life. I came here for some peace and quiet. The first time she messes that up, she's gone. Make sure she understands that."

"Of course," Vince said smoothly. "Anything else?"

"Yes," Roe snapped. "When is she coming?"

"She's booked on a flight tomorrow night."

Roe couldn't help smiling ruefully. Vince was as ruthlessly efficient as ever. "Okay," he said. "I'll be waiting."

"Can you pick her up at the airport?" Vince was really pushing it now. The whole conversation, in fact, was uncomfortably reminiscent of Roe's youth and his arguments with Vince about looking after their mother.

"I don't have a car," Roe reminded him, determined to draw the line here. "Look, I made it here on public transportation. No reason why she can't."

"You know the way," Vince pointed out. "And you speak the language."

"Not really," Roe replied repressively. "If your rock star can't even make it from Palermo to Sontara on her own, you'd better just put her in cold storage until you've recovered."

"Sontara *is* my idea of cold storage," Vince muttered. After a few more minutes of arguing, Vince finally accepted that his brother wouldn't relent. "All right, have it your way. Keep an eye out for her — even you must know what she looks like. She should be there the day after tomorrow. And try to be a little civil."

"Sure," Roe said blandly. "She's a *star.* " He heard Vince, sigh and added, "Vince? Just one more thing."

"Yes?" Vince asked warily.

"Look after yourself."

*T*wo days later, Roe vehemently cursed the rock star as he rented a car in Trápani, the ancient western port of Sicily, and drove to Palermo, steeling his nerves against the insanely every-man-for-himself nature of Sicilian traffic. Nowhere, not even in Cairo, had he ever seen kamikaze driving to compare with the highways and byways of his mother's native land. As experienced as he was at driving vehicles through all sorts of terrain in any kind of weather, he nonetheless hated driving in Sicily. And it was all Gingie's fault that he was risking his life on the highway today, rather than napping on the beach below his house or helping Zu Aspanu in the lemon groves.

The phone call had come while he was pushing his lunch around his plate, finding he still couldn't work up much enthusiasm for food. Vince had given Roe's phone number to Gingie before putting her on the plane in New York. Her confused explanation of the situation in English was not much clearer to him than the one he received in Italian from some customs official who took the phone away from her. As he struggled to understand the man, Roe wished once again that he had made more of an effort as a child to learn Italian.

Despite his fluency in several languages, Roe's Italian was terrible, a sluggish mixture of proper Italian, Sicilian dialect, and phrases and pronunciation that were unique to the island of Sontara, all of it haphazardly acquired during his childhood and used only on his infrequent visits here.

Consequently, he had no idea what kind of situation he would encounter when he reached the customs office where Gingie was being held. He could at least communicate simple phrases with reasonable accuracy, so he knew they understood that he was coming right away. Having missed the daily ferry which ran between Sontara and the port of Trápani, he had convinced one of his cousins, a local fisherman, to take him over to the mainland after siesta. Nevertheless, it was getting late by the time he arrived at Punta Ráisi Airport outside of Palermo and found Gingie.

She was sitting cross-legged atop a desk in an overcrowded and underdecorated office full of men in various uniforms — local police, national police, soldiers, and customs officials. There was also, Roe noted with a sinking feeling, a photographer present. Presumably someone already knew Gingie was in Sicily.

As Vince had predicted, even Roe, who maintained as little contact as possible with American pop culture, could easily pick Gingie out of the crowd. She was currently absorbed in plunking out notes on a small laptop keyboard, apparently battery-operated.

He had, of course, seen videos and photographs of her before. But nothing, he decided, could quite prepare someone for the reality of Gingie. As he entered the office and introduced himself in his halting Italian to a beleaguered-looking official, Gingie looked up. When she realized that her savior had arrived, she slid gracefully off the desk and sauntered toward him.

She was tall, he noticed, only three or four inches shorter than his six foot two. She was slim, with long, coltlike limbs, small, high breasts, and a narrow waist that flared out to arousingly feminine hips. Her skin was alabaster white, as smooth and perfect as a baby's. Her wide mouth was painted fire-engine red, and her eyes were as blue as the sky over Sontara. They were framed by thick black lashes and coal black eyebrows which were a startling contrast to her short, fluffy, blond hair. The effect was unexpected and undeniably appealing.

"Gingie?"

"Yes," she answered him. "You're Prospero Hunter?"

He grimaced. "Call me Roe." Every time someone said his full name, he regretted his mother's romantic streak.

"I'm so glad you're here," she said in a rush, her voice low and honey smooth. "I can't understand what's wrong."

Roe's glance flicked down her body. Even if the customs men hadn't recognized her, her outfit alone would have singled her out for attention. Why the hell hadn't Vince told her to dress a little less conspicuously? She wore an improbable outfit that appeared to be entirely one piece, from the turned-up collar and tight, long-sleeved bodice, all the way down both tightly sheathed legs to the pointed toes and silver heels encasing her feet. Made of some shiny black material, the outfit was highlighted by numerous provocatively placed zippers that obviously had no practical purpose, but which certainly sparked the imagination.

He drew his eyebrows down in what he hoped was a forbidding frown. She damn well better have packed something a little more appropriate for a holiday in rural Italy. Assuming he could even get her released.

"Let's find out what the problem is," he said tersely.

"They seem concerned about my remedy box," she offered.

"Your what?"

"*Prego, signore,*" said a uniformed man at that moment, leading Roe over to a suitcase sitting on another desk. An Oriental wooden box lay open next to it, its former contents carefully lined up on the edge of the desk.

Roe noticed the suspicious-looking contents of a clear plastic bag right away. He didn't need the customs official's carefully phrased comments to understand the problem.

"For the love of God," Roe exploded, whirling to face Gingie again. "Couldn't you have left this junk behind?"

Her blue eyes widened. "Well, I tried to bring only what I was sure I'd need," she said hesitantly, "but Letitia says it's best to be prepared for the worst."

"Who's Letitia?" he demanded.

"My sister."

Her sister was her supplier?

"She's a homeopathic doctor," Gingie added innocently.

"A homeopathic doctor?" he repeated blankly. He glanced at some of the other bags that lay on the countertop, as well as at the little vials of liquid. A strange feeling came over him. "Gingie," he said in a strained voice, "what is this stuff?" He pointed to the bag whose contents appeared to be illegal.

"Gosh, I don't remember the name," she said despairingly. "Letitia gave me a list, but I seem to have lost it. But I'm sure I remember what everything's for," she added.

Clinging to his patience, he asked, "What's it for?"

"That? I'm supposed to infuse one ounce in boiled water to prevent..." She tilted her head and looked almost shy for a moment before concluding, "Digestive irregularities."

Roe rubbed a weary hand across his forehead. He had come all the way from Sontara for this? "You mean to say that these are all just . . . dried medicinal plants and ground-up roots?"

"Yes, of course. And tinctures. What else would they be?" After a brief pause her eyes went saucer-wide. "Oh, no! You mean, they thought . . ."

Roe nodded, wondering how she could be so naïve.

"Well, really!" She was clearly insulted now. "After all the 'just say no' public service messages I've done, it never even *occurred* to me that they'd think I was —"

"I guess they don't watch MTV, Gingie."

She looked around at a half dozen suspicious, watchful faces. "No, I guess not," she agreed meekly. "So what do we do, now?"

"What do *we* do?" He'd like to put her on the next plane back to New York. However, Vince would probably keel over. So he said, "You're going to go sit in that corner and stay out of trouble while I clear this up."

"Ah." She glanced doubtfully at the corner he had pointed to, then frowned and said carefully, "Maybe I should help you."

"Sit," he ordered.

He spent a half hour settling the matter with another customs official. Mercifully, this one spoke some English. Breaching the language barrier one way or another, Roe was able to explain the nature of the misunderstanding. Things could have been resolved even sooner, but Roe understood the Sicilian love of drama, so he patiently pleaded and argued, knowing that this was probably the most fun his opponent had had all day.

Finally, they concluded the discussion and shook hands on good terms. As someone bundled up Gingie's belongings and closed her suitcase, Roe told her they were free to go.

"What about my remedies?" she asked, hopping to her feet.

"They'll have to stay here, Gingie."

"What? But what if I get sick?"

Roe sighed, inexplicably beguiled by the combination of dismay and innocent trust in her impossibly blue eyes. To his surprise, he heard himself promise, "I'll see if we can get them back after someone examines them, okay?" It shouldn't be too difficult; he dealt with customs officials all the time.

She gave him a brilliant smile, the kind that had made her one of the most photographed women in America. "Thank you, Roe!"

At that moment, a flash went off. Roe turned swiftly, and another flash went off right in his eyes. Blinking, he snarled at the photographer, using an extremely rude phrase he had learned from Zu Aspanu. The man beat a hasty retreat, but Roe wondered uneasily where those photos would appear.

"Let's get out of here," he said, longing for the peace and quiet of Sontara. He hoisted her heavy suitcase easily. "Is this everything?"

"No," she answered. "The rest of my luggage is over there." She pointed to an enormous pile of luggage: five, mismatched suitcases, two garment bags, and a footlocker.

"Which one is yours?"

"All of them," she said, as if that should be obvious.

"All of them?" he repeated incredulously. When she nodded, he turned on her in exasperation. "Gingie, are you planning on moving permanently to Sicily?"

"No, but Vince said I should expect to be here a whole month." Seeing his annoyance, she added defensively, "I tried to bring only the essentials."

He thought he felt a headache coming on. "All right," he said in defeat, "I'll find a porter."

Whenever Roe was at Punta Ráisi, it always seemed to him that there was only one porter for the hundreds of passengers milling around. After finding the man, Roe slipped him an outrageous tip in advance so he wouldn't chicken out when he saw Gingie's pile of luggage. When they returned to the spot where Gingie awaited them, Roe saw that she had added an outlandish, wide-brimmed, black hat to her outfit, and a huge pair of sunglasses that obscured her blue eyes.

"What the hell are you wearing?" Roe said rudely.

She tilted her sunglasses down to give him an uncertain look. "This is my disguise," she explained. "Vince said I should try not to attract too much attention."

Roe returned her look as a feeling of helpless despair seized him. It was going to be a very long month.

Two

*I*t took a lot of time and creativity to load Gingie's luggage into the car that Roe told her he had rented in Trápani. Gingie felt kind of bad about that, but she wasn't used to planning trips. Someone else had taken care of her luggage for years, so she'd had no way of foreseeing what kind of difficulties a woman could encounter when travelling solo with six suitcases, two garment bags, and a footlocker. Organizing the practical details of a journey had always been someone else's job. Music was hers.

After the luggage was loaded but before they got into the car, Roe paused and said patiently, "There's no *cambio* on Sontara, you know."

Gingie squinted, wondering if he was testing her. At last she admitted, "I don't know what you mean."

"There's no *bureau de change,*" he amended, as if that should be obvious.

Gingie frowned in puzzlement.

"Money changer," he said with a trifle less patience.

His scowl made him look a lot like his mother, Adelina Marino. Gingie supposed he had inherited his astonishing good looks from the Italian film actress. He had raven-black hair, lustrous and wavy, and his skin was darkly tanned. His face was strong and square-jawed, its hard masculinity made faintly exotic by high cheekbones that were reminiscent of his mother's.

He was tall, too. Gingie didn't have to look up to many men, but she had to tilt her face up slightly to look him in the eye. His eyes, she thought, were unique. Unlike the Sicilian chocolate-brown of Vince's eyes, of their mother's eyes, Roe's eyes were a light brown that glittered with intriguing amber highlights. They were passionate, intelligent, secretive eyes . . . .

"Gingie?" he prodded, the sandpaper quality of his voice giving it a shiveringly sexy timbre.

"Money changer?" Her eyes widened. "That's right! I have traveler's checks!" She drew them out of her fringed purse with a flourish. "This is so exciting!"

He sighed. "As I said, there's no money changer on Sontara, so you'd better change some money as long as we're here."

"Will you help me?" she requested.

"Help you?" he repeated in surprise. "Gingie, I know you've done two world tours, Vince sent me postcards. Surely this can't be all that new to you."

"But it is," she insisted. "I've never been abroad by myself before. Vince or the tour manager or someone else handles all these details for me when I tour. I just work."

He stared at her, his eyes glittering with speculation. "Are you telling me that you — a grown woman who's probably been to as many countries as I have — don't know even the simplest practicalities about foreign travel?"

Gingie bit her lip and shook her head, feeling stupid. She should rise to the challenge, she chided herself. This was precisely the sort of experience she was looking for, exactly the kind of encounter she had decided she needed when Vince had broached the subject of this trip.

"You're right," she said bravely. "I'm a grown woman. You wait here. I'll go change my money." She turned to go.

"Gingie," he said in a strained voice. She turned back to him. He indicated the carry-on bag sitting on the passenger seat of the car. "I noticed your passport's in there. You'll need it."

"What for?"

"Identification," he said somewhat hoarsely.

"Oh," she said. "Oh, yes. Of course." She hadn't needed to identify herself to anyone in over three years. It was an interesting prospect. She rifled through her bag, found her passport, and promised, "I'll be right back."

"I'll go with you," he offered resignedly.

She flashed him a smile, glad that he had apparently decided to be nice again. "No, that's okay. This will be good for me."

He looked at her strangely, but gave an acquiescent shrug. She felt his eyes on her back as she headed into the airport.

"*I* think we'll have to spend the night in Trápani," Roe warned her as they drove westward along the dark highway. He added by way of explanation, "Sontara's pretty isolated."

"Yes, Vince said you can only reach it by ferry once a day, and there aren't even any cars when you get there." She frowned suddenly. "Oh, gosh. What'll we do about all my luggage?"

"We can load it up on my uncle's donkey cart."

She glanced at his profile. His eyes were glued to the road. The drivers around them seemed a little irresponsible, but Roe drove with such skill and concentration, Gingie felt perfectly safe. "How did you get off the island today? Did you catch the only ferry?"

"No, it was too late. A relative brought me over, but it's too dark for him to come out now. We'll check into a hotel in Trápani tonight and catch the ferry tomorrow morning."

Gingie nodded and continued to study him in the dark, searching for a resemblance to his father. She had met Jordan Hunter once at an awards ceremony in New York. There wasn't a whole lot of physical similarity between them, even accounting for their age difference. Jordan Hunter was slick and refined, while Roe was brawny and broad-shouldered. She had noticed his strength, not to mention his impressive supply of muscles, while he was loading the car. Far from being heavy and square, however, he was long-legged, narrow-nipped, flat-bellied, and limber. His body gave the impression of being designed for absolute efficiency, a combination of speed, strength, and stamina.

His mouth, she decided, was pure Italian, full-lipped and sensual. She'd like to see him smile.

She had already noticed the marks on his face and wondered about them; it looked as if a woman had raked her nails down his cheek with considerable venom. It was another feature that made him look dangerous, mysterious, and tough, like the unruly black waves of his hair, the bulging muscles of his shoulders, and the unexpected flecks of amber glowing deep in his watchful eyes.

All in all, Roe Hunter seemed surprisingly unlike his brother, her manager, who was shorter than Gingie, heavyset, and balding. Roe possessed a curious quality of stillness, as dynamic as a cat waiting to pounce, whereas Vince was a bundle of nervous energy, always talking, always moving, always worrying. Despite everything, though, she kind of missed Vince now, Gingie realized with a faint pang of homesickness. She missed Milo, Sandy, Letitia, and the band as well. She'd never been on her own before.

A car swerved directly in front of them without warning. Roe applied the brakes, his arm flying out protectively in front of Gingie. Her gasp caught in her throat, then they resumed normal speed. He put his right hand back on the wheel. His hands were smooth and long-fingered, but she had felt the toughness of his palms when he had taken her elbow at the airport.

Gingie sighed. He was an incredibly attractive man. It was just as well she was so accustomed to celibacy, she reflected, or she might let herself be seriously distracted by him. As she gazed at him in the dark, exhaustion from the long trip and the preparations preceding it finally overcame her. She curled so that her whole body faced Roe, then rested her head against the back of the seat and closed her eyes.

"*H*ey, Gingie, wake up."

His rough whisper seemed to come only a moment later. Then she realized that they weren't moving. She rolled her head slightly and opened her eyes. They were parked on a city street. She made a sleepy sound and let her head loll forward until it connected with something warm, hard, and surprisingly comfortable. Roe's shoulder, she realized hazily. He felt nice.

She felt the faint puff of his laughter against her hair. "Didn't you sleep on the flight?"

"No," she sighed. "I can't sleep on planes. Too cramped."

"Well, if you can pull yourself together for just a few minutes, we'll get a bed," he promised. He paused, then cleared his throat. "I mean, we'll get two beds. I mean, I'll get you a bed, and then . . . Gingie," he concluded sharply, "wake up."

Gingie sat up quickly. She didn't want to be a burden to him. "Is there a hotel near here?" she asked sensibly.

"Across the street," he answered, getting out of the car as fast as if she had tried to bite him. "We can leave the luggage here for a few minutes."

She followed him across the street and into the lobby of an elegant hotel. "How long was I asleep?"

"About an hour."

"I'm hungry."

"We'll get something to eat after we check in."

"Vince said Sicilian food is good."

"Best in the world," Roe said, glancing uneasily around them.

"What's wrong?" she asked.

"We're attracting a lot of attention."

"Oh." She glanced around as they continued across the lobby to the reception desk. "Maybe I should have worn my dark glasses."

She thought he stifled a laugh. "I don't think those really help, Gingie."

"Oh." She shrugged. "Maybe you're right." People stared at her everywhere she went, and it had been that way for years. She didn't expect that to change just because she was on vacation.

Roe got the attention of the desk clerk and was apparently asking if there were two rooms available. The clerk, however, recognized Gingie and cut Roe off with an exultant cry. The man clasped both Gingie's hands excitedly and started speaking very rapidly. Gingie smiled and nodded, then glanced at Roe.

The clerk spoke rather tersely to him. Anger and humor warred for a brief moment in Roe's face before humor won out. With a faint quirk of his lips, he said, "He's ordered me to translate everything he says"

"What's he saying?"

"That it's an honor and a privilege to have you here, and that he will make the hotel's finest suite available to us."

Thanking the man with her best smile, Gingie obligingly signed several autographs before Roe could commence the process of checking in. The clerk humbly asked for Gingie's passport, explaining apologetically that it was the law in Italy. She handed it to Roe, who looked at her speculatively a moment later when the clerk handed it back to him.

"Virginia Potter?"

"That's my real name," she told him. "My family always called me Gingie. When I signed with Vince, he said I didn't need a last name. He said I was unique."

"Yeah, I see his point," Roe said mildly. Once they had signed the register, Roe added, "I'll get a porter to bring in your things. Can you manage with just one or two bags tonight?"

"Yes, I'll show him which ones I need," Gingie offered.

"I'll have him put the rest in storage until morning."

In the end, Gingie couldn't quite remember what she had put where, so she had the porter carry up one garment bag and one suitcase, hoping she would find whatever she needed for the night.

A little unique in her approach to life? Roe thought murderously as he ascended to the suite with Gingie. He would kill Vince for this, assuming Vince was well enough to be killed next time they met.

Gingie was a child, an infant, an innocent, some kind of social mutant from never-never land. She was, according to her passport, thirty-one years old. Yet she had never cashed a traveler's check, despite having gone on two world tours. She seemed to think that it was reasonable to bring more luggage with her to Sontara than Princess Di had taken on her honeymoon. And she was apparently under the delusion that she was dressed inconspicuously in that crazy, skintight, black-and-silver outfit.

How had Vince ever thought Gingie could travel from New York to Sontara without a Secret Service escort? And how, Roe wondered, did she manage to be so incredibly naïve?

Roe had heard enough of Vince's stories to know how people lived in the world of rock and roll. It was just as chaotic, hedonistic, and wildly insecure as life in the Hollywood film community. The temptations of drugs, booze, and easy, empty sex were plentiful in both worlds.

Roe closed his eyes in remembered pain and began to strip in the privacy of his bedroom within their suite. He hesitated when he heard a soft knocking on the door.

"Roe?" Gingie's voice was melodic and smooth. "I'm going to shower and change before we get dinner, if you don't mind."

"I'm going to shower, too," he called back. After a moment of silence, he continued undressing. She was going to change? Thank God. After his initial surprise at her outfit, the thing he had noticed most about it was how outrageously sexy it made her look. It would have looked absurd on most women, and downright mean on others; but somehow, on Gingie, it looked provocative, intriguing, alluring, and just too damn good for his peace of mind.

Well, sure, he thought, unsnapping his jeans and shedding them. Of course she was sexy. He should have expected that. Very few performers became as famous as Gingie without an abundant supply of sex appeal.

But he *had* expected to be immune to it.

He grimaced at the thought, then stepped into the bathroom to turn on the shower. Roe had spent most of his youth among the so-called beautiful people. Growing up in Hollywood had made him cynical; it had also taught him to be immune to commercial sex appeal, even when it came in such astonishing proportions as Gingie possessed.

So he really didn't understand why Gingie made him want to stare, just the way everyone in the lobby had stared at her earlier. He stepped under the shower spray, letting the hot water ease his tension. He'd been attracted to plenty of women, but his attraction to this one made him uneasy. It had been a long time since he'd allowed himself to be bowled over by sheer sexual magnetism, by a pair of hips that swayed like . . .

He adjusted the water to make it a little colder.

*W*hen he met her at the door of their elegant suite, he finally understood why she had genuinely believed her black outfit and crazy hat were inconspicuous.

"Is something wrong?" she asked, noticing his expression.

"Oh, no. You just might be a little overdressed," Roe suggested blandly. "This is a provincial city in an isolated region, Gingie."

"Italians are very fashionable people," Gingie protested. "I want to look my best."

"Have it your way."

He opened the door and began trying to help her through it. Her dinner clothes were actually rather simple, just a celery-green pair of silk trousers and a sleeveless shirt of the same material. The pièce de resistance, however, was her wrap. It was shaped like an octopus, complete with eight arms, all of them alarmingly animated as she shifted and wriggled to get them through the door without hurting herself.

Composed of a variety of charming sea colors, Roe figured Gingie's cape was probably the first thing he'd seen in over ten years that left him virtually speechless. The funny thing was, once he got used to it, he thought Gingie looked rather wonderful in it. How did that woman manage to make something so outlandish look so right?

As they walked down the street together toward a *trattoria* he knew, he supposed it was the graceful, elegant, unconsciously sensual way she moved that made her eightarmed aquarian outfit look perfectly natural. It took some time to pull her arms out of it once they reached their destination, and he had to tip a waiter generously to find a place for it where it wouldn't get damaged while they were eating.

"You see?" Gingie told him as they were seated at a candlelit table. "All the people here like my cape."

"I should have guessed," Roe agreed dryly. "Sicilians love anything that dramatic. And the octopus is one of their staple foods, as well as being a symbol of many things. Including," he advised her, "the Mafia."

"Really?" Her excited exclamation made him grin unexpectedly.

That's it, Gingie thought, staring at him. His broad smile was the one physical trait he had inherited from his famous father. It was uninhibited, alluring, playful, and sensual. All the things that made a woman want to be alone with a man.

His teeth were awfully good, too, just about as good as her own. "You should smile more often," she told him.

"I do, when I'm not keeping rock stars out of jail on smuggling charges."

She smiled, too. "It makes you look a little like your father."

He stopped smiling instantly. "So Vince told you who my father is?"

"He jogged my memory, that's all. It's not a secret, is it?" She frowned. "I mean, I don't see how it could be."

"No, I guess not."

"I read some of those Hollywood biographies when I was a teenager, and you were quite a baby sensation. Adelina Marino for a mother, the most beautiful woman in the world according to some people, and Jordan Hunter, the British singer, for a father. Everyone thought you'd get into films, too, when you were a boy."

He looked away. "Luckily, my mother kept me out of the limelight. She wanted to raise Vince and me the way she had been raised. That wasn't possible, of course, but she tried."

"How was she raised?" Gingie asked curiously as the bottle of local wine Roe had requested was placed before them.

"Quietly. On Sontara"

"Really? So we're staying in her family's old house?"

"No. My uncle lives in the house they grew up in. After her first husband — Vince's father — died, she began building her own villa on the sea there. That's the one Vince and I own." He started to pour some wine into her glass.

She stopped him. "I don't drink."

He glanced at her, his guarded gaze showing a flicker of surprise. "Oh."

"Don't like the taste," she admitted. "Milo says any truly sophisticated woman should cultivate a taste for wine, caviar, and Mahler, but I don't like any of them."

The name triggered something in Roe's memory. "Milo?"

"Milo Wake, my keyboard player. Please, go ahead," she added, when he didn't pour any wine into his own glass. "Just because I don't drink, that shouldn't stop you from having some."

"I, uh, don't drink, either," he said.

"Oh. Maybe we should give the bottle back, then." When the waiter returned a moment later, Gingie urged Roe to order for her rather than translate the menu. "I eat almost everything," she assured him. "And order lots. I'm kind of hungry."

He was glad later that he had taken her at her word. For a slim woman, she could consume a truly amazing quantity of food. Having polished off the olives and chickpea fritters Roe ordered as *antipasti,* Gingie proceeded to demolish a plateful of pasta with clams, a sautéed filet of swordfish, a salad of fresh fennel and tomatoes, half a loaf of crusty bread, a selection of cheese and fruit, and a pastry stuffed with ricotta cheese. In between mouthfuls, she kept up an animated stream of chatter about her trip from New York, charming him against his better judgment with her speculations about her fellow passengers, all of whom she considered possible spies, jewel thieves, top-level diplomats, or fugitive lovers. She had a fertile imagination — not to mention an astonishing appetite.

"Do you always eat like this?" Roe asked warily, thinking there probably wasn't enough food in his house to hold her for more than one day.

"Oh, no. When I'm on tour, I eat a whole lot," she explained earnestly. "To keep up my strength."

He considered this. "Do you want anything else?" he asked with a strange feeling of awe.

She appeared to think about it for a moment before deciding, "No, I've heard people often gain weight on vacation, so I'd better watch it."

He blinked. "On vacation?"

"I've never been on vacation before. This is very exciting. I can hardly wait to get started," she said cheerfully.

Dumbfounded, Roe gazed into those guileless eyes. No, not guileless, he thought angrily. Thoughtless. His brother was about to undergo heart surgery, and this silly blond rock star was bleating about how happy she was to be on vacation! He was annoyed to realize he'd gotten so caught up in her dinner performance he hadn't even asked her about Vince.

"How's my brother?" he said sharply.

"Fine." Gingie took a sip of her fourth glass of freshly squeezed orange juice and added, "He says I mustn't cause too much trouble because you've been through a bad experience and might not be feeling very patient right now." Her long-lashed gaze offered sympathy.

Roe leaned back, as if a few more inches of physical distance could diminish the dewy effect of those eyes. "What else did he say?" he asked suspiciously.

Her expression changed again, reflecting amusement this time. "Oh, lots. He says you're the black sheep of the family. But don't let that worry you. I've been the black sheep of my family since I was born, and it hasn't held me back."

"No, I can see that," he agreed without warmth.

If she noticed his tone, she chose to ignore it. "Vince says he can't understand why a man of your background and talents continues to actively avoid the limelight, hiding on Sontara on those rare occasions when you're not living out of tents in godforsaken backwaters of unpronounceable countries."

"That sounds remarkably like Vince," Roe said wearily.

"Oh, it's a direct quote," she assured him mischievously. "But he also says you're his little brother, absolutely trustworthy, and he loves you."

Roe poked at his food and tried not to show how foolishly touched he was by Vince's effusiveness.

"Your poker face isn't perfect," Gingie said softly.

He glanced at her sharply, surprised. She gave him a delighted smile.

"Your eyes give you away, Prospero Hunter." She leaned forward and studied him with interest, engulfing him in a fragile, crystalline moment. "They're yours. Yours alone."

"Mine?" He heard a husky catch in his voice. How did she do this to him?

"They're not your mother's eyes, or your brother's, or even your father's." Her voice dropped almost to a whisper. "Nobody has eyes like you."

"Don't . . ." he began. He trailed off, his mind a daze. What did he want her not to do?

She ended their mutual staring contest to search the rest of his face. Without warning, she lifted her hand and brushed her fingertips across his cheek, a casual, unselfconscious touch. A feminine touch. Soft, delicate, enticing.

"What happened?" she asked.

"What?" he said blankly, trying to repress an unbidden image of those soft, elegant fingers brushing across his lips.

"Who did this?" She traced the gradually healing scratches made by Lisa's fingernails.

Hating the memory, he suddenly grabbed her hand and pulled it away from his face. "A fight with my little sister. My father's daughter with Candy Jirrell," he clarified.

Gingie was wide-eyed. "She attacked you?"

"She wasn't herself at the time," Roe said vaguely.

"Wow, and I thought *my* sisters could be temperamental.

He was hotly aware of her hand folded in his, cradled against his chest. Her bones were long and aristocratic, her skin so soft he had to stifle the impulse to stroke his way up her wrist and forearm to the creamy white shoulder exposed by her delicate silk shirt. He stared for a moment, mesmerized by her pale throat, the delicate shell of her ear, and the strong line of her jaw. His gaze shifted hungrily over her, too greedy to rest on any one feature. He met her eyes again and felt a powerful quiver of longing, sharper than desire, deeper than attraction.

Holy Mother, I don't believe this. No wonder the woman had two platinum albums and had sold out every concert on her last world tour, according to Vince. Roe yanked his gaze away from hers, plopped her hand unceremoniously back in her lap, and tersely signaled to the waiter for the check.

Whatever sorcery Gingie possessed, it was certainly potent. He would have to remember that, he thought fiercely as he doled out money for their meal. It had never occurred to him before her arrival that he would have to monitor his self-control. He was starting to fear she might pull him out of his apathetic depression in the most uncomfortable way possible.

Gingie cheerfully signed menus and place mats in the *trattoria* before they left, having been recognized, and profusely thanked the owner for her wonderful meal. Like all Sicilians, the owner loved a woman who could eat, so he gave Gingie a bouquet of flowers, a package of beautifully sculptured sweets made from almond paste, and a warm invitation to return as soon as possible.

As Roe and three waiters helped her back into her tentacled cape, he began to realize what made Gingie harder to ignore than the other famous, gorgeous women he had known in such abundance. Her cheerful absurdity and bizarre impracticality made a man lower his guard, the way he would for a playful puppy. Then, when he wasn't looking, she suddenly turned back into that sultry singer who had burned up the concert stages of half the world with her heat waves.

As he escorted her outside and down the street, he recalled Gingie's videos that he had seen on his last trip to the States, some three years earlier. She didn't employ the scantily-clad, hip-grinding, heavy-handed performance techniques of some of her peers. She didn't need to. When Gingie looked directly into the camera, you felt the back of your throat tighten. When she lifted the microphone to her mouth and sang, your breath got shallow. When she danced, you wanted to have her all to yourself, far from the crowds that always seemed to surround her.

"What are you thinking about?" Gingie asked suddenly. "You seem kind of tense."

"Nothing." He tried to force his body to relax. Like most things he had tried to force in his life, it didn't work.

Three years ago, he mused. Gingie had already been on top for a couple of years by then, but Roe had never even seen a picture of his brother's sensationally successful client. It had been a family weekend in Connecticut, Roe having stopped off on his way from Zanzibar to LA, and he had only watched the videos out of politeness and at Vince's insistence.

He'd been impressed by Gingie's talent. The range and depth of her honey-smooth voice could easily have ranked her among some of the finest jazz singers who had ever lived, but Gingie had chosen rock, the voice of her generation. Fully clothed and without ever making one overtly sexual gesture, she sang and danced for the camera with a sizzling hot sensuality that burned a man's senses. There was nothing indecent in any of the videos, yet Gingie seemed to perform on the razor's edge, poised so dangerously, so boldly over the mysterious abyss of female sexuality that Roe's gaze had been glued to the screen, waiting for some elusive revelation, waiting for her to expose the secrets so lushly promised in her expressive eyes, her graceful hips, her daring songs.

Of course, it was all illusion. He'd seen it manufactured his whole life. He might respond to it during a performance, but he had learned never to let himself forget that such images were carefully, skillfully produced, often with a lot of technical support. So he had complimented Vince on having found such a strong performer, and that was that.

Now, in the flesh, he found Gingie unsettling, surprising, disturbing, unexpected. Zu Aspanu probably had a saying for this strange feeling, Roe reflected wryly. The old man had a saying for every occasion.

Wary of the heat Gingie stirred in him, Roe resisted her only other effort at conversation as he escorted her into the hotel and followed her toward the elevator. Talking to her only made him sink into those lush blue eyes and start fantasizing about hearing her rich, vibrant voice whisper to him in the shadows of his bedroom. It was better to maintain his distance, he decided. He had a lot of experience at that, too.

When they reached the suite, Gingie, as if sensing his mood, said tentatively, "I have to call home. Would you show me how?"

He nodded and picked up the receiver. Perhaps because it was late at night, getting an international line was easier than usual. He handed the phone to her. "All you have to do now is dial the area code and number," he explained.

He was already unbuttoning his shirt and opening his bedroom door, painfully aware of the intimacy of sharing this suite with her, when he heard her say, "Hello, Sandy? It's me!"

He closed the door behind him and leaned against it in the dark. Something clicked in his memory. Something about Gingie's scandal and the reason Vince had to get her out of the public eye while he was laid up.

Sandy . . . That was it. Sandy Stephen was a name that even Roe, so far removed from the scene, had heard many times. Barely twenty-one and already extremely controversial, the young man had been at the top of the music charts since his meteoric rise to fame a couple of years earlier.

And he was widely publicized, Roe realized with a jolt, as the constant companion of a woman ten years his senior — Gingie.

Roe frowned, trying to remember more. In his mind's eye he saw a blurry photograph in black-and-white. Gingie was at the center of some kind of scene.

He had read the article, peripherally interested in it because Gingie was Vince's client, Vince's livelihood. Roe started stripping off his clothes, folding them neatly out of habit as he moved around the darkened bedroom. He had been so tormented by worry, fatigue, guilt, and sorrow because of his sister, that he had paid scant attention to the story at the time.

The headline, he remembered now, had said something about Gingie alienating her fourth record company in a row. That was probably what had made Vince so determined to put her in cold storage while he was hospitalized, Roe reflected. A slight smile touched his mouth as he finally remembered the photograph: Gingie dumping a plate of food over the head of an important record company executive. No, that definitely wouldn't appeal to Vince's sense of humor, even though it had lightened Roe's dark mood at the time.

Roe recalled that the tabloid article had speculated wildly about Gingie, her escort Sandy Stephen, her "live-in lover" Milo Wake, and the somewhat intoxicated record company executive.

Roe shook his head as he went into the bathroom. Why was he even surprised? And as for the vague sense of disappointment he felt . . . Hell, hadn't he learned his lesson long ago? Wasn't Gingie exactly the sort of person he'd spent most of his adult life avoiding?

He heard her calling his name just before he slid into bed. Annoyed, he pulled his jeans back on and opened the connecting door. She stood by the phone, her fluffy blond hair and alabaster skin highlighted by the Mediterranean moon peeking through the windows. She had shed her octopus outfit without his help this time. She looked surprisingly young and innocent as she twisted her hands and met his eyes.

"Were you asleep?" she asked, her voice like molasses.

"Not yet." The faint swell of her small breasts gleamed like ivory. She released her breath, and the smooth mounds quivered slightly. He suddenly wanted to touch them. His throat went dry.

"Oh. I'm glad." She smoothed her palms down her thighs and stared at him, confusion evident in her expression. "That you're not asleep, I mean."

He recognized what was happening to him. He was less sure about what he saw happening to her. If this unsought desire wasn't simple for him, it looked monstrously complicated for her. "What do you want, Gingie?" he asked carefully.

"I'm sorry to bother you again, but I didn't really see what you did the first time."

"What I did?" he said blankly. He narrowed his eyes. She licked her lips.

He was going to sleep alone tonight, he assured himself. There was no question of getting tangled up with her. No question at all. He stalked forward, feeling his heart thud heavily in his chest. Her gaze dropped to his bare chest and its tangle of black hair. He heard her draw in a quick, sharp breath. *I'm not going to do this,* he promised himself, lying shamelessly.

"What you did to dial overseas," she said huskily.

"Overseas?" he repeated stupidly. He stopped stalking and just stared.

She nodded. "I need to call Milo." There was a long silence between them. She held out the receiver at last. "Will you help me?"

He dialed the phone for her and went back to his room without saying a word, wishing desperately that Vince had stowed his keg of dynamite somewhere else.

Three

The island of Sontara lay about thirty kilometers northwest of Trápani. Unlike the nearby Aegades Islands, Sontara attracted so little tourism that it had no hotels. To accommodate the island's few visitors, Signor Sellerio and his family moved in with his mother-in-law every year from May until September and rented out the rooms of their fine new seaside home to tourists.

Roe explained all of this to Gingie as they approached Sontara on the ferry — a rather grandiose word, Gingie thought, for the aging cargo boat that transported the two of them to the island along with the daily mail, dry goods, and some rather odorous livestock. This was, she assured herself, an adventure.

Since the island was only fifteen square kilometers and had only one road worthy of the name, there were no cars on Sontara. When Signor Sellerio heard that Don Ciccio was planning to buy a Fiat and transport it to the island by ferry, he had convinced the town council to pass an official law against automobiles on Sontara. Don Ciccio — Roe pronounced it Chee-cho — had countered this move by buying a golf cart. Now no one knew what to do, and Don Ciccio enjoyed lording it over lesser individuals as he puttered around Sontara in his new status symbol.

Gingie smiled as Roe told her this, and other tales, with the polite, skilled, impersonal charm of an expert tour guide. She almost felt as though she should tip him. She supposed he was still annoyed about having to come all the way to Palermo for her yesterday. She was trying to make it up to him by being extra nice, but it wasn't having much effect on him.

He had been curt with her at breakfast and so remote for the rest of the morning that she began to feel she might just as well be traveling alone. Now, as they saw Sontara in the distance, he had finally begun speaking to her again, but he sounded like a stranger and scarcely glanced her way.

"Electricity only came to the island in 1978," he explained.

"Hollywood must have been quite a change for your mother, after growing up here," Gingie said conversationally.

"Even Rome was a big change after Sontara," Roe said. "She went there after World War II, to find work. But the Italian film industry was so devastated by the war, she practically starved."

"And then she was discovered by Vince's father, who made her a star in America," Gingie added, for the story was well-known. While in Rome, the American film producer had seen Adelina Marino's picture and, intrigued by it, had arranged a screen test for her. A month later, he brought her back to Hollywood with him, this young Sicilian woman who only spoke a dozen words of English, and he became her producer, friend, mentor, and, finally, husband.

Apparently wanting to avoid discussing his mother, Roe pointed into the distance. "Look, you can see the village now."

Gingie squinted at the island and saw a collection of colorful little houses all facing out to sea, a small stone cathedral, and a harbor full of fishing boats. It was all surrounded by a beautiful backdrop of rocky cliffs, green mountains, and pristine white beaches.

"Oh, it's beautiful!" Gingie said enthusiastically. She gripped his arm and smiled up at him, wanting him to know how much she liked it.

He looked down at her, his expression showing pleasure for a brief, unguarded moment. Then he went still, like a wild animal, and stared at her quietly, a cautious, bemused light glittering in his gold-flecked eyes. The wind whipped through his shiny black hair and made his collar flutter, giving him a slightly piratical look beneath the startlingly blue Mediterranean sky.

Gingie felt it again, that unexpected, belly-clenching, breathless feeling she had experienced last night when he had come out of his bedroom wearing only his tight, lowslung jeans. The sensation made her feel helpless, quivery, confused. It made her want to melt against him. Startled and a little alarmed, she looked to him for guidance. He was, she had no doubt, more experienced than she.

Roe shook off her touch as if she'd burned him, then he stepped away. "There are about six hundred people living on the island," he continued in a flat, stoic voice, "and they maintain a pretty traditional way of life." He gave her a hard, meaningful look before adding, "Vince assured me that you wouldn't disturb that."

She blinked at him. "How could I disturb the traditions of six hundred people?"

His impatient gesture suddenly made him look very volatile and Italian. She remembered his shoulders, gleaming darkly in the moonlight, and the blue-black hair curling crisply on his chest. She remembered the taut, washboard muscles of his stomach, and the quivering electricity that had sprung up unexpectedly between them in the shadows. She had been stunned and nervous, because she was normally in complete control of her libido.

"Let me put it another way," he was saying. "I've come here for some peace and quiet, for a breathing space. The only reason I agreed to let *you* come here was because Vince assured me you wouldn't get in the way, cause trouble, create scenes, be demanding, make a nuisance of yourself, or disturb the tranquility of Sontara in any way." His voice was sharp enough to cut through stone.

"Oh." Gingie was hurt by his attitude. Vince had led her to believe that she would be slightly more welcome than this.

"You've already caused trouble at the airport —"

"That wasn't my fault!" Gingie protested.

He lowered his head for a moment. "No," he conceded at last, surprising her. Vince never admitted that anything *wasn't* Gingie's fault. "I guess it wasn't. But I told Vince and I'm telling you. If you make trouble even once, I'm sending you right back to him."

Gingie tried to be understanding. After their conversation last night, she had connected the scratches on Roe's face to Lisa Hunter's recent, nearly fatal overdose in LA and subsequent admission into a drug abuse clinic. Lisa Hunter's position as Candy Jirrell's daughter had inspired public interest in the incident, even more so than Lisa's own sporadic acting career. Gingie wished Vince had been more specific when he had said Roe had recently been through a bad experience. She would have thought twice before intruding.

"Well, I'm here now, and Vince hasn't given me a return ticket yet," she said aloud, "so we might as well make the best of it. I'll try not to bother you."

He looked at her strangely, as if waiting for her to say something else. Gingie couldn't think of anything else she wanted to say, so she just returned his stare evenly.

"Okay," he said at last. "As long as we understand each other."

There were a lot of people waiting for the ferry when it docked: handsome, sturdy, sun-darkened men waiting to unload the cargo, two uniformed middle-aged men waiting for the mail, and a wrinkled old farmer awaiting the live-stock. Everyone seemed to know Roe, which Gingie supposed was natural on such a small island. People stared at her curiously, and a few tried to speak to her, but Roe hustled her through the crowd as efficiently as Vince might have done.

He stopped dragging her along behind him when they finally reached a snoozing donkey that was harnessed to a rickety wooden cart. Two old men, one fat, one skinny, both wearing tweed caps, stood next to the donkey, shouting at each other so loudly Gingie wondered how the donkey could sleep.

Roe interrupted the men, speaking a peculiar mixture of English and the musical, vaguely garbled language that Gingie had learned comprised his unique version of Italian.

Both old men stopped shouting long enough to greet Roe and stare at Gingie. She stared back, liking their wrinkled, friendly faces and dark, secretive eyes. The fat one stepped forward and kissed Gingie's hand in a courtly gesture that almost made her laugh. Sensitive to the old man's feelings, however, she gave him her best smile. He murmured something, then poked Roe imperiously, obviously ordering him to translate.

Roe sighed. "Gingie, this is Don Ciccio. He welcomes you to our humble island and says that you honor us with your presence."

Before she could respond, the skinny old man next to Don Ciccio elbowed him out of the way, barking rudely, then removed his cap and squinted at Gingie. "The pleasure is mine," he said in thickly accented English.

"This is Zu Aspanu," Roe explained.

"Zoo?" Gingie said doubtfully.

"Zu is Sicilian for *zio*, " the old man said, as if that should be obvious.

"It means 'uncle,'" Roe clarified.

Gingie smiled and shook Zu Aspanu's hand, wondering at the strength in his thick, gnarled fingers. "I'm so happy to meet you," she assured the old man. "If someone could get my luggage, I have something . . ." She let the sentence trail off and looked back toward the ferry.

Roe, Don Ciccio and Zu Aspanu conferred in Italian, then the two old men ambled over to the dock, growling at each other the whole way. Roe watched his uncle for a moment, and Gingie's throat swelled at the open fondness she saw in his expression when he thought she wasn't looking. It made him look so different, younger and more tender.

She was accustomed to attractive men, of course. Her world was full of them. However, she was also accustomed to being virtually immune to them, so Roe's effect on her was unexpected and unfamiliar. Maybe it was because he was so clearly different from any other man she had ever known. He was what Milo would call an enigma. Or rather, he tried to be, but those expressive, glittering, golden-brown eyes gave him away more often than she suspected he liked.

Roe was, Gingie realized, too much like what she imagined when she wrote her songs or gazed into the eye of the camera. There was a force in him that was as powerful, seductive, and mysterious as the echoes of an empty coliseum when she did her sound checks. There was a quality in him that was as bright and exciting as the roar of the crowd when Gingie appeared on stage.

Did Vince realize how attractive his brother was? Petting Zu Aspanu's donkey and avoiding Roe's gaze, she supposed that if Vince knew, he had probably assumed it didn't matter. He had said Roe was absolutely trustworthy, which Gingie knew meant, among other things, that Roe wouldn't put moves on her. And after nearly ten years of working together, Vince knew Gingie's habits, too. She slept alone. Always. Of course, that never stopped Vince from complaining about the way Gingie was usually at the center of scandal and gossip despite the austere life she led.

What was she supposed to do? she fumed again, as she had been fuming for months now. Did Vince expect her to kick Milo out of her apartment when he had no place else to go? Did he want her to simply reject Sandy's clinging friendship, when the shy boy was so overwhelmed by his sudden, meteoric rise to fame that he wasn't comfortable talking to anyone on the East Coast except her? Should she tell her oldest sister Camilla to bury her principles and stop getting arrested in demonstrations for various causes?

Was Gingie supposed to stop living the way she wanted to just because everyone watched her now? Did she have to come out with a public statement every single time a little misunderstanding — like the one at customs yesterday — occurred? If *she* could tolerate the tabloids, the scandal, the gossip, and the image she had unwittingly acquired, why should Vince be so apoplectic about it? All Gingie wanted to do, all she had ever wanted, was to write and perform her songs.

Gingie sighed and scratched the donkey's ear. She tried to see things from Vince's point of view, since she had, in fact, just alienated her fourth record company. She and Vince had fought about that, too. Gingie saw this vacation, taken all by herself with no supervision, as Vince's vote of confidence after the long power struggle she had begun with him on her thirtieth birthday. His invitation to spend a month in the house he co-owned with his brother was, she believed, a peace offering.

She recognized it as a compromise, too. Vince knew where she was, and he knew his brother was with her. Gingie wasn't opposed to compromise, as long as it was made in good faith.

Gingie and Roe had to wait quite a while for her luggage. The captain of the ferry unloaded it last of all since, according to Roe, Zu Aspanu had managed to mortally offend the man last week with some comment about his boat. Then Don Ciccio made an enormous production of having Gingie's belongings loaded onto his golf cart, whereupon he drove it over to Zu Aspanu's donkey cart and had it transferred from the golf cart to the donkey cart while the donkey eyed the proceedings warily.

"Better late than never, eh?" Zu Aspanu said at last to Gingie as he helped her find a comfortable position on top of her footlocker. The old man then rounded the cart and, after giving the donkey an encouraging pat, took the beast's halter and began leading him down the road. After checking to make sure Gingie was comfortable, Roe joined his uncle, chatting with the old man as they walked beside the donkey on the dusty road out of town.

They cut between two mountains and entered a lush valley full of vineyards and vegetable fields where eggplant, lettuce, and tomatoes grew. Lemon, orange, and ancient olive groves covered the steep hillsides, and the occasional farmer they passed waved to them and called out greetings. They finally cut through a field and turned onto a high, narrow coastal road, where the natural scenery was even more breathtaking. They passed a few houses, and Gingie noticed colorful laundry fluttering in the breeze and children playing under their mothers' watchful eyes. The sun was warm, and the breeze was balmy and soothing after the lingering chill of early April in New York. No wonder Vince had told Gingie she would love Sontara.

Roe's villa, when they reached it, was simple but serenely beautiful. A two-floor white stone structure, it was set away from the road and protected from prying eyes by dozens of trees and shrubs. Bougainvillea, oleander, and wisteria climbed over the walls and through the archways in a riot of bold color, and the entire house perched on a cliff overlooking a beautiful stretch of beach and sea directly below.

The interior was airy and romantically old-world, with high ceilings, heavy wooden doors, stone tile floors, and a delightful array of Italian furniture, art, and handicrafts. The room that Roe politely told Gingie would be hers had a vast bed, a beautifully ornate baroque dresser and armoire, a rustic hope chest, and french doors leading out onto a small balcony overlooking the sea.

As they unloaded her luggage and carried it into her room, Gingie enthused about the villa, the flowers, and the view.

"Hollywood can't hold a candle to Sontara," Zu Aspanu assured Gingie as they all stood on the main terrace behind the house and admired the view.

"You've been there, haven't you?" Gingie asked. "Vince says you were often in America during his childhood."

"*Sì*," the old man confirmed.

"Zu Aspanu even worked in Hollywood as a cameraman for a dozen years and made good money," Roe offered, "but in the end, he came back to Sontara to marry and settle down."

"Home is where the heart is," Zu Aspanu said serenely. When he started to leave, Gingie remembered she had brought something for him. She told him to wait on the terrace for her, went to her room to rifle through her suitcases, and returned a few minutes later with her offering.

Zu Aspanu expressed great pleasure that she had brought him a gift, insisting that she shouldn't have bothered. When he opened the box and peered inside, there was no doubt about his genuine delight. "Peanut butter!"

"I asked Vince what I could bring his family, and he told me how you had developed a taste for peanut butter in America, and how difficult it is to find in Sicily." Gingie was pleased her gift had gone over well. It had seemed a strange thing to bring.

"Look!" Zu Aspanu pulled out one of the four sixteen-ounce jars Gingie had brought him and showed Roe. "Skippy Extra Crunchy! My favorite! This beats the band!"

Roe smiled. "You've found your way into my uncle's affections," he told Gingie.

"I thank you from the bottom of my heart," Zu Aspanu said enthusiastically. *"Molte grazie, signorina."*

A few minutes later, the old man carefully loaded his treasure into the donkey cart, climbed onto the small wooden bench now vacated by Gingie's luggage, and snapped the reins to set the donkey off at a brisk trot.

After he had disappeared, Gingie turned to Roe and smiled. "I like your uncle."

"He likes you." Roe's voice sounded almost grudging.

She followed him back into the house. There were four bedrooms, but except for hers, they all looked as if they'd been empty for some time. "Where do you sleep?" she asked.

His expression was carefully blank. "I gave you my room. It's got the best view. It used to be my mother's room." He led her out onto the balcony and pointed to a small cottage about a hundred yards from the house, built into the side of the cliff. "I'll sleep in the guest cottage."

"But Roe, that's silly! You don't have to move out of this beautiful villa just because I'm here. There's plenty of room." Before he could respond, she added, "I've already promised not to bother you."

He looked a little bemused. "It's not that, Gingie. I told you that people on Sontara are very traditional. They wouldn't approve of our staying here together without supervision. Even my staying in the cottage will only be acceptable because everyone knows me and trusts my, uh, sense of honor."

Gingie was surprised. "That's amazing. This is the last decade of the twentieth century."

"It takes a while for Sontara to catch up with the trends," he said wryly.

"Look, Roe, if I worried about what people said or thought, I would have lost my mind years ago, as I keep telling Vi —"

"I don't want to argue about it," he said dismissively.

Gingie pursed her lips for a moment, but decided to let it go. This was his turf, after all, and maybe he knew best.

"I've got to go. You'll be all right on your own now, won't you?" he said.

"Where are you going?"

"I've got to go back into town."

"But it took nearly an hour to get here," she protested. He must surely be a little tired.

"It's only about fifteen minutes on my bicycle," he assured her. "Zu Aspanu's grandson, Gaspare, will take care of maintenance while you're here. I've just got to find someone to cook and clean everyday. I usually only have the house cleaned once a week when I'm here alone."

"But, Roe, I don't —" Gingie started to object.

"See you later." He left abruptly.

*T*he girl Roe hired to do the cooking and cleaning was Signor Sellerio's youngest daughter, Maria, who spoke only a few words of English. Though pretty, she was so painfully shy that even Gingie, who seldom had trouble talking to anyone, couldn't get her to do anything more than blush whenever she spoke to her.

Roe's cousin Gaspare, the seventeen-year-old who took care of the gardens and general maintenance around the villa, was extremely modern and a great fan of Gingie's. He was also obsessed with everything American and goodnaturedly confided to Gingie, in his colloquial English, that he thought Roe was a fool for abandoning the life to which he'd been born.

During the next three days, Gingie unpacked and settled into her new environment, read a great deal, started writing a new song, and explored the grounds around the villa.

By her third afternoon on Sontara, Gingie figured she was about as relaxed as she could get, short of being unconscious, so her naturally active nature began to assert itself. She glanced at her watch as she lazed on the terrace and realized that she had been lying in the shade for nearly two hours. Lying in the sun was out of the question with her fair skin, and anyhow, a person could only lie around for so long before feeling the need to stimulate and be stimulated.

So, of course, her mind turned to Roe. He was, after all, very stimulating. He had more or less avoided her ever since their arrival seventy-two hours ago, speaking to her only when absolutely necessary, and remaining polite but uncommunicative during the meals they shared.

Although she hardly knew Roe, Gingie could tell he was suffering from classic symptoms of depression. His dark complexion and strong bone structure didn't readily show fatigue, but Gingie could see it etched in the fine lines around his mouth and eyes.

He napped often during the day, stretching out on their sun-drenched beach, wearing only a pair of cutoffs. The first time she had seen him, she thought he looked like some hero from an ancient legend washed up on the sand, his golden, leanly muscled body sprawled out with unconscious sensuality while Gingie jogged past him. Once, while doing her sit-ups, she had seen him awaken with a start, as if troubled by nightmares.

She had also noticed that he didn't seem to sleep at all at night. Having only recently come off another concert tour, as well as having flown halfway around the world, she had woken up twice on her first two nights in the house and once last night. On every occasion, Roe was either walking along the beach in the middle of the moonlit night or standing on the terrace, gazing out at the endless expanse of sea.

Except for last night. Last night he had been gazing up at her bedroom window. As she emerged onto the balcony, wearing only a gossamer gown designed to look like a spider web, a sudden tension had sprung up between them, binding them together in a moment of breathless, wary silence. She hadn't been able to see his eyes in the darkness, only the shape of his body, taut with apparent surprise at her sudden appearance, and the bold highlights of his strong face in the moonlight.

Breaking the bond at last, Gingie had backed into her bedroom and paced uncertainly for nearly an hour. Was he lonely? Did he want to talk? To have a companion? She wanted to go to him, to share the dark night with him, but she was afraid he would want things she couldn't offer him.

In addition to his restlessness, Roe wasn't eating well. Maria came in every morning to tidy the house and would stay just long enough to ensure that Roe liked whatever she had prepared for lunch. Although he always assured her that the food was delicious, which it certainly was, he was eating as lightly and disinterestedly as he had. that first night in Trápani. Since Gingie *always* ate well, Maria's feelings hadn't been hurt yet.

Compassion wrenched Gingie's heart. Roe was undoubtedly depressed about his sister. Perhaps he blamed himself, since he had tersely admitted at lunch that he was in her Los Angeles house with her when it happened. Or perhaps the incident had dragged up all the unhappy memories of his mother's death some ten years earlier.

She sipped her freshly squeezed orange juice and considered how to help Roe. Since her entire career was about helping people enjoy themselves and escape from their problems for an evening, or even for the space of a song, there ought to be something she could do for Roe.

She supposed his active avoidance of her was his way of telling her he didn't want her company. Yet his behavior last night, and the haunted look in his gold-flecked eyes, called out to her.

Maybe, Gingie thought, they could help each other. After three unprecedented days of solitude, she was at loose ends. She leaned over the terrace railing and looked at Roe stretched out on the beach far below. A quick spurt of excitement shot through her, and she realized her motives weren't entirely blameless.

"It's okay," she assured herself blithely. "I can handle this. I've come too far to stumble now." With a decisive nod, she picked up her hat and trotted down the narrow stone stairs carved into the cliff, which led to the beach.

*I*nstinct warned him he wasn't alone even before he awoke. Years of living either in the bush or in crime-ridden third-world cities had made him alert to his surroundings even when asleep. Slowly gathering his senses about him, he pinpointed the intruder without even changing the cadence of his breathing. A moment later, his hand shot out and he seized a soft, slim wrist.

Roe opened his eyes, squinting against the bright afternoon sun. "What are you doing?" He tried to sound reasonable as Gingie gaped at him in surprise.

"Waking you up, I guess," she said. "Please, Roe, I may need that wrist again someday."

"I'm sorry." He was. He changed his grip and massaged the tender flesh he had grasped so forcefully. She was wearing some absurd little outfit that looked like a lot of leaves sewn together. A huge straw hat shadowed her delicate skin from the sun. She looked ridiculously pretty. Aware that the way he was touching her had made her eyes go smoky, he dropped her wrist and closed his eyes again, throwing his arm across his face.

Every outfit she wore was more bizarre than the last, and she just kept looking better and better in them. He resented it. He resented her presence. He resented the way his cousin and his uncle had already fallen under her spell, the way shy Maria had already started imitating her gestures, the way she made him feel hot and alert when he wanted to go back to feeling dull and fuzzy. But most of all, he resented the way her helpless irrationality made him want to look after her.

"I don't know what to do next," she said suddenly.

"Next?" he heard himself ask.

She sighed. "I've never been on vacation before. I mean, I've read, I've lain in the shade I've eaten, I've slept . . ."

He knew she'd been reading. He had noted the books with more than a little surprise: *Prime-time Television: The Popular Imagery of Sexual Oppression* and *Early Evidence of Social Structures in Anatolia.* Even disregarding stereotypes about rock stars, it wasn't what he would have expected her to bring along on a seaside holiday.

"What else do people do on vacation?" she asked.

"You've really never done this before?" he asked suspiciously. He had assumed she was exaggerating.

"Not since I was a child. And it was different then."

"Yes, I suppose so," he agreed dryly.

"All I've done for the past thirteen years is work." She touched his shoulder lightly, sending a ripple of unwelcome excitement tripping through him. "Maybe you could help me, Roe."

The hesitant, honey-smooth sound of her voice was shredding his resolve to simply ignore her, to keep in mind that she was an unwelcome guest thrust upon him by his brother. He found himself, contrary to all logic, wanting to do something for her. Why did she violate his self-imposed lethargy this way?

"Well, Gingie," he said at last. "Maybe you'd like to take a tour of the village. We could even have dinner there."

"Oh, could we, Roe?" She sounded as excited as a little kid. She seemed to have no reserve, no self-protection. Where the hell had Vince found her? "That would be wonderful!"

Roe stifled a smile and picked himself up off the sand in one smooth, easy motion. He reached for her hand and pulled her to her feet. Her broad-brimmed hat bumped his face and she laughed.

"Sorry," she apologized. "It's so cumbersome, but it keeps the sun off me."

He nodded, still holding onto her hand, liking the firmness of her grip, the openness of her brilliant smile, the healthy sparkle in her eyes. "I'll bet you burn easily," he said.

She rolled her eyes. "I don't burn, I stroke."

"Then maybe we should get out of the sun." Still holding her hand and feeling unsettled, as if she were cracking the ice inside him, he led her to the steps carved into the cliff. "You first. Watch your step."

He conceded a few moments later that it might have been a mistake to let her go up first. The smooth flexing of her calves and thighs as she climbed the steps ahead of him, the exuberant sway of her hips, and the rhythmic motion of her arm along the ancient wooden railing were too hypnotic for his peace of mind.

Suddenly she stopped. "Oh, look!" she cried, pointing out to sea. Roe followed her gaze and saw a sleek, trim sailboat gliding gracefully across the water. "Isn't that beautiful?"

She glanced back at him just as he rose another step. They both froze, suddenly caught by this thing that had been playing cat and mouse with their senses. His bare chest nearly touched her naked shoulder, their faces were only inches apart; and their legs brushed enticingly.

"Yeah," he agreed huskily. "Beautiful."

Gingie swallowed and continued to stare at him, her smile slowly disappearing. Her face was scrubbed clean, and her mouth was slightly red even without lipstick. Her fluffy blond hair looked soft and silky in the breeze. Her black lashes fluttered down, hiding the confusion in her expression as her lips parted and her head tilted ever so slightly.

He felt the ache of desire spring to life inside him, and with it, so many other aches. The need for tenderness pierced his tough hide, and he touched his finger to her chin, wanting to be gentle because she seemed so vulnerable, and because he bore too many scars to play rough anymore.

He leaned forward slightly, taking the moment slowly, hoping he would find a way to talk himself out of this. His lips touched the trembling warmth of hers, and he squeezed his eyes shut, steeling himself against the impossible sweetness of her mouth.

Suddenly he felt her hand on his shoulder, her fingers gripping him hard, the pressure pushing him away. He lifted his mouth a fraction of an inch away from hers, hungry for the taste of a real kiss, wondering what was wrong. The glitter in her eyes and the flush in her cheeks were familiar to him, yet somehow special and unique because these age-old signals were coming from Gingie this time.

He let his question show in his eyes. She wasn't afraid or reluctant or insulted. On the contrary, she was breathing quickly and looking at him as if she would melt in another minute. But the hand on his shoulder continued to firmly push him away.

"I don't . . ." she began. She licked her lips and closed her eyes, as if tasting him in her imagination. He wished she wouldn't do that. "I don't ever . . ." She smoothed her hand down his arm and then suddenly, with a little sound, snatched it away from him. "I just don't."

She turned away from him and marched resolutely up the stairs, leaving him gazing after her.

Don't what? he wondered.

He continued to stare blankly, thinking he might be better off just going back down to the beach and being depressed again, when a faint ringing alerted him. The telephone. "Thank God," he muttered. The phones hadn't worked since Gingie's arrival, making their isolation together seem that much more pronounced.

Hoping the caller would be Vince, who wasn't scheduled for surgery until tomorrow, Roe climbed the rest of the way up to the terrace, thinking of all the things he was going to say to his brother about this arrangement. Gingie had only been here a few days, and already she was disturbing his solitude, not to mention his peace of mind. And there was no reason to suppose things would get any better.

When he reached the house, however, Gingie was finishing the conversation. She hung up the phone and faced him.

"That was Milo," she said brightly. "He and Sandy have just arrived on Sontara. They're wondering if we could come and get them?"

Four

"*I didn't* invite them," Gingie explained to Roe as they bounced along in Zu Aspanu's donkey cart. They had hiked over a steep, rocky hill to the old man's farm to borrow it, and now the valiant donkey was hauling the two of them along the dusty coastal road to the village.

"Then what are they doing here?" Roe demanded.

"I don't know. Maybe it's just a coincidence." The absolutely disgusted glitter in his eyes made her amend, "Maybe Vince sent them but couldn't notify you. After all, this afternoon is the first time the phones have worked since we got here."

Roe grunted. That appeared to be his way of ending the argument, which was fine with Gingie. As far as she was concerned, it was a big relief that Milo and Sandy were about to become their constant chaperons.

She remembered the hot, soft feel of Roe's lips brushing lightly against hers, the tension rippling through his body when she touched him, the look of open longing in his usually guarded gaze. Gingie shivered, trying to get control of herself.

"Are you cold?" Roe asked. He sounded irritable. When she shook her head, he added, "You should have changed clothes."

She was still wearing her little leafy, green outfit. "I'll be all right."

"I mean you shouldn't be wearing that to the village. You should have your shoulders and legs covered, Gingie."

"Is there anything else you'd like to criticize while you're at it?" Gingie said in her first flare of temper since arriving on Sontara. Why were people always trying to tell her what to do?

Roe looked a little taken aback by her tone. He clicked the reins and frowned at a spot between the donkey's ears. "I'm sorry," he said at last.

Gingie glanced at his profile. It was more than a polite phrase spoken to head off another argument. He actually meant he was sorry he had criticized her. Without thinking, she put her hand over his. "I'm sorry my friends have upset things."

He lowered his gaze to look at her hand as it covered his. Gingie felt the tension come flooding back into his body, which he held rigidly still. Her breath caught in her throat. He smelled of soap and sea air, his skin was warm from the sun, and he was wrapped in some kind of raw energy that set off sparks inside Gingie. His hands were long and slim, almost aristocratic except for their dark, sun-stained color and slight roughness. His grip tightened on the reins and his voice sounded slightly hoarse when he said, "Gingie . . ."

Their eyes met suddenly. She was fascinated by his face, so starkly beautiful, so exotically masculine, with the sad memory of Lisa Hunter's scratches healing on one cheek. His shoulders were very broad, too, broad enough for her to lean on, wide enough to shelter her. She felt a tugging deep inside, something so unfamiliar and compelling, she forgot about everything else.

Without stopping to think about the consequences or foolishness of her actions, she slid her palm over the hair-roughened skin of his forearm and up to his shoulder, which was covered by the sleeve of his simple cotton shirt. She stroked the thick muscles she found there, bewildered by her own excitement. He was terribly strong, far stronger than she was, despite her rigorous workouts and exemplary lifestyle.

"Gingie, this isn't . . ." His words trailed off and his thick, black lashes fluttered down when she rubbed her palm over his biceps, marveling at his coiled energy.

"What do you think you're doing?" His voice sounded feeble and half-hearted, low and a little gravelly, a thrilling contrast to the raw power he kept tightly leashed under her exploring fingers.

Dropping the reins in his other hand, he brought it up and placed it over hers, stopping her stroking. His grip was almost rough, it almost hurt. Almost. Behind his wary and confused expression, she could see so clearly that he wanted to be gentle. Something inside her chest starting filling up, feeling heavy and hungry at the same time.

"I . . ." She stopped speaking, her mind a blank. Her gaze dropped to the warm curve of his lips. "I want . . ."

One wheel of the donkey cart dipped into a hole, tossing Gingie against Roe. She braced her hand on his shoulder to steady herself. With her legs and chest pressed against him for an instant, with her face inches from his, with his breath stirring her hair, she suddenly knew what she wanted. And it was, of course, absolutely out of the question. She wasn't about to sacrifice her years of carefully cultivated abstinence and all that went with it for *anyone*.

Gingie snatched away from him as if she'd been burned. She avoided his eyes, ashamed of her naïveté. How could she have thought she could handle this? Hadn't her number-one single, *Playing With Fire*, assured everyone that you should never do it?

Aware of his bemused stare, she finally said, "I want to hurry. They've probably had a long trip."

He picked up the reins without comment and, stonefaced, returned his attention to the donkey.

Gingie concentrated on staring at her sandals. She was astonished. When was the last time something like this had happened to her? She frowned. Nothing precisely like this had *ever* happened, actually. After all, Roe hadn't even come on to her. She had awkwardly stumbled into that sticky place all by herself, without any significant help from him. Just his existence was apparently stimulus enough to make Gingie behave in a manner she had successfully avoided under the most seductive of circumstances with the most attentive of men.

She recalled a French film star who had sent so many roses to her hotel suite every day for three weeks that there finally wasn't enough room for all the band's instruments anymore. She recalled a guitar player who, when describing all the delightful things he would do to her if she let him, had used words she'd never heard before and couldn't find in the dictionary. She had later put those same words into a song which became her second top-ten single. She recalled a British writer who had sent her an invitation to dinner and then tried to feast on *her* toward the end of the evening. But she couldn't recall anyone like Roe.

There were men who wanted to put a notch on their bedpost representing rock 'n' roll's infamous blond legend, and there were eager fans who wondered what an hour alone with her would be like. But thanks to Milo and Sandy, there had been fewer annoying — if flattering — distractions in the past couple of years. And the more famous and wealthy she became, the fewer men were prepared to approach her, particularly when she always had an escort anyhow.

So the unsettling distraction Roe caused was surprising and disturbing, not to mention inconvenient. Fortunately, however, he appeared to be quite a gentleman. She would have to try, though, not to count on that again. Her oldest sister, Camilla, would tell her how irresponsible that was.

*T*he sun was casting a westerly orange glow over the village by the time Roe and Gingie reached the port. Gingie's friends were easy to find, since Milo had already started a card game with a number of men hanging out on the main piazza, and Sandy was surrounded by women and girls requesting his autograph.

Roe couldn't believe it. Sontara, the sleepiest, quietest place in the world, a place so remote and untouched that even his mother had been able to hide here, was turning into a three-ring circus. He had to get rid of these people. However, he obviously couldn't throw them out of his house without talking to Vince first. And Vince would be in surgery tomorrow and then convalescing the rest of the week. Stoically accepting that he was stuck with Gingie and her friends for the time being, Roe helped Gingie out of the donkey cart.

"Milo! Milo!" Gingie cried, running across the piazza and flinging herself into the musician's arms.

Roe followed slowly. Talk about mixed messages, he thought. Back there on the coastal road she had touched him as if she owned him, looking at him with the vibrant interest of a woman who's ready, willing, and waiting. Then, for absolutely no apparent reason, she had changed her mind and scooted to the far edge of the rough wooden seat, refusing to touch him or look at him again. What was he supposed to do, he fumed — pretend that he wasn't affected by it? When confronted with a woman like Gingie, he concluded, no one's self-control was *that* good.

And now there she was, flinging herself into Milo Wake's arms and hugging him as if he'd just rescued her from a fate worse than death. She would drive Roe nuts if he let her, so maybe it was just as well her friends had shown up uninvited.

Seeing Roe approaching them, Gingie gestured to him and said, "Milo, this is Vince's brother."

"Prospero Hunter?" Milo asked.

Roe sighed. "Call me Roe."

"Milo Wake." The long-haired blond musician whipped off his rose-colored glasses long enough for Roe to see his eyes, then shook Roe's hand enthusiastically. His pale blue gaze was friendly, intelligent, and bloodshot. Judging by the crow's-feet around his eyes and the thinning hair over his forehead, Roe figured Milo must be well into his forties. He wore shabby jeans and a psychedelic shirt, his clothes partially covered by his oversized black vinyl trench coat. Roe noticed a saint's medallion shining on a chain around Milo's neck. Seeing the direction of his gaze, Milo grinned and said, "Joseph of Cupertino, patron saint of air travelers." With a slight shudder, Milo added, "I never leave home without it."

"You don't like flying?" Roe guessed.

"Milo *hates* flying," Gingie corrected. "The last time we flew from Tokyo to San Francisco, Milo got so hysterical he passed out in the airport and had to be revived at thirty thousand feet." She hugged Milo again. "I'm so surprised to see you!"

"Frankly, I'm a little surprised to be here." Milo sighed. "Four whole days without you, Gingie. It was so reminiscent of my life before we ever met. Peaceful, practical, predictable. Hardly anything really confusing, chaotic, or incomprehensible happened for four whole days."

"I know what you mean," Roe muttered.

"Yeah, I guess you do," Milo said sympathetically. Their eyes met and, despite considerable reservations, Roe found himself already liking the keyboard player.

"If it was all so pleasant," Gingie said, "then what are you doing here?"

"It was peaceful, I should say, until Sandy came over yesterday, panic-stricken because he hadn't heard from you since your phone call from the hotel in Trápani."

"Oh, poor Sandy," Gingie said. She explained to Roe, "He's used to talking to me every day."

"I see," said Roe, not seeing at all.

"So he insisted I contact Vince and get your phone number. And when we discovered that the phones here weren't working, Sandy became hysterical and insisted we come find you at once. Well, his manager was furious, since Sandy's got television appearances all next week, but that didn't deter the boy. Since I couldn't really let him go alone . . ." Milo shrugged and wrapped one hand around his saint's medallion, his talisman against the evils of air travel. "So here we are. Hope you've got room for us, Roe."

"Oh, sure, the more the merrier," Roe said, keeping his voice carefully neutral.

"Sandy!" Gingie cried as the other man spotted her and, breaking away from his adoring fans, came over to join them. Her reunion with the young rock star was far less exuberant that her reunion with Milo. Sandy simply came to her side like an obedient cocker spaniel, took her hand in his, and stood there looking placid. Knowing that Sandy used some of the most graphically sexual lyrics and images in pop music, Roe was surprised at the boy's mousy, self-effacing manner.

Gingie introduced him to Roe. Sandy shook Roe's hand and murmured a polite greeting, shy as a schoolboy. He was much blonder than Milo, and his clothing was the height of fast-lane chic, based on what Roe had seen in California on his recent visit. Sandy was tanned, blue-eyed, and very good-looking. Despite Roe's irritation with the whole scene, he couldn't help but be amused at the adoring stares directed at Sandy by more than fifty women who had suddenly found reasons to be in the piazza. Even Signor Sellerio's foul-tempered old mother-in-law was girlishly trying to catch Sandy's eye as she paraded back and forth with her empty shopping basket.

Having been introduced, Sandy made no effort to participate in the rest of the conversation, apparently content to silently stick like glue to Gingie's side, holding her hand and looking around without ever meeting anybody's eyes.

"How's my brother?" Roe asked Milo.

Milo said quickly, "In good spirits. Optimistic. His wife is a hell of a woman, you know."

"Yes."

"We were going to eat dinner in town," Gingie said eagerly, apparently unconcerned about Vince's health. Roe wanted to shake her. "Does that sound good to you?" she asked Milo.

"Sure, Gingie. I just want to get our luggage taken care of."

"There's Don Ciccio!" Gingie exclaimed. "I'll handle this."

Roe watched with surprise as Gingie extracted herself from Sandy's clinging hand and, with a reassuring smile, left them all to go greet Don Ciccio.

"*Gingie's* going to make arrangements for the luggage?" Milo said disbelievingly. "That's a switch." He glanced at Roe. "I guess this trip is having a maturing effect on her."

Roe shrugged noncommittally, baffled by all of them. He'd seen a lot of things in his life, but he had never before seen two men as willing to share the same woman as Milo and Sandy apparently were.

"Sandy," Milo said, "I've had a very hard day, so we're going to go sit at that café over there where I can get a stiff drink." His words were carefully enunciated, as if he were speaking to a child he didn't know well. "Joining us, Roe?"

After a quick glance at Gingie, who was cheerfully assaulting the language barrier with Don Ciccio, Roe inclined his head, and the three men pushed past the crowd around them to find an empty table in the café. It was, Roe realized unhappily, the first time he had ever even *seen* a crowd on Sontara.

After they sat down, Roe ordered a cola for himself and a freshly squeezed orange juice for Gingie, and Milo ordered himself some whiskey. As they all waited for Gingie, Sandy sat in apparently contented silence while Milo recounted the more dramatic aspects of their journey for Roe's benefit.

"The airport here is amazing," Milo said. "Ever been to Jakarta?"

Roe nodded. "Once. Yeah, I know what you mean." Despite everything, Roe supposed Milo — whose descriptions of the flight made it clear that he really was phobic about flying — must truly love Gingie if he was willing to come all this way for her. He supposed that the nonstop traveling life of a musician could account for some of Milo's more obvious eccentricities.

"Everything's taken care of," Gingie assured them when she joined them a little while later. "Don Ciccio is hauling everything up to the donkey cart in his golf cart. Then that boy who hasn't been allowed to date Signor Sellerio's third daughter says he'll load it up for me."

"I'm amazed, Gingie," Milo said frankly.

"I'm hungry now," she said.

"Naturally," Milo replied.

"Shall we eat at that little place over there?" Gingie pointed to a *trattoria* on the other side of the piazza.

"We really shouldn't," Roe said.

"Why? Isn't the food any good?" Gingie asked.

"Oh, the food's great," Roe assured her. "But there are only two *trattorie* on Sontara, and I have to be careful not to show any favoritism. Since I ate at that place the first night I got here, I'm really kind of obliged to eat at Signora Gambarossa's place tonight."

"Ah, the politics of village life," Milo murmured. "So where is this other place?"

Roe pointed over Milo's shoulder. "That way. About fifty yards past Santa Cecilia."

"Past who?" Gingie asked.

"The cathedral," Roe explained.

"Santa Cecilia?" Milo exclaimed. "We've got to go inside!"

"I didn't know you were so interested in architecture, Milo," Gingie said.

"No, you don't understand. Don't you know who Saint Cecilia is, you ignoramus?" Milo demanded.

Gingie shook her head, so Roe said, "The patron saint of musicians."

"Really?" Gingie was intrigued. "Let's go see it."

They finished their drinks, then Milo unabashedly made Gingie pay the tab. "She's richer than the rest of us," he explained pragmatically to Roe, "and she always forgets that things have to be paid for, even in this best of all possible worlds."

Gingie frowned abstractedly at the table until Sandy nudged her. "Oh, Sandy, would you mind walking ahead a little? There's something I have to discuss with Roe," she said.

Sandy nodded and trotted off to join Milo. Gingie rose from her seat and slowly walked across the piazza with Roe, apparently oblivious to all the gazes that followed her leaf-clad figure.

"Something wrong?" Roe asked mildly, noticing the look of concentration on her face.

"Well, we've stayed in a hotel, eaten out, ridden in a ferry, and rented a car. You've hired a maid and bought lots of groceries. I just realized that all of that must have cost money, but I haven't given you a single cent." Her wide blue eyes sought confirmation. When Roe inclined his head, she said, "I can certainly pay my own way, and I don't expect you to feed my friends now that they're here. I'll take care of all those bills. Why didn't you say something before now, Roe?"

He shrugged. "I figured I'd just sort out the money thing with Vince, Gingie."

She made an impatient gesture. "No. *I* want to do it. That's why I came here, to get away from all that."

"All what?"

"My life being controlled by other people."

He squinted doubtfully at her. "You really want to manage your own money?"

She thought about that for a moment. "No, I guess not. I'm . . . I'm not very good at practical things." She seemed to think she was revealing a well-kept secret. A moment later she said suspiciously, "I have a feeling you're laughing at me."

"I, uh, I'd already noticed that reality wasn't your strong point, Gingie."

"Oh." She sighed in frustration. "Maybe we should compromise. You tell me every few days how much I owe you for all the expenses you incur because of me, and I'll give you the money."

"That's . . . very trusting of you, Gingie." Where had Vince found her? he wondered again.

"Vince said I could trust you," she said matter-of-factly.

This time he let himself smile. It was just too hard to stay irritated with her. "Done, Gingie. I'll figure it up tomorrow and let you know how much you owe me so far. Okay?"

"This is a big step for me," she admitted.

Roe glanced down at the harbor, where Don Ciccio was having Sandy and Milo's luggage loaded onto his golf cart. "You can handle it," he assured her.

She smiled uncertainly. "Thanks, Roe. Nobody else thinks so."

He stopped walking and turned to face her, realizing she meant it. Despite her disruption of his solitude, despite the sudden appearance of two of her lovers on his sleepy little island, despite the way she teased his senses, he suddenly knew an overwhelming desire to fill the need he felt in her. Against all reason, he desperately wanted to give her a piece of what he sensed she needed.

"Then they should take a closer at you, Gingie. By the time you were in your mid-twenties you had already climbed to the top of the most heartbreakingly competitive business in the world. And you've kept a fickle public coming back album after album, concert after concert for five years."

She shook her head disrnissively. "That's what I'm good at."

"And you've even stayed sane while doing it. Nobody does that without enormous personal resources. Believe me, I know."

She smiled softly at him and took his hand. "Maybe you do."

"You can do whatever you want. You just haven't focused your attention on practical matters the way you've focused it on your music. But I'll bet you can do anything you set your mind to."

"Anything?"

"Of course. Just look at how much you've done already."

"So you think I could get better at practical things?"

He grinned. "At least a little better. If you want to."

"I do," she said emphatically. They started walking again. "I was lucky to meet Vince all those years ago, just like I'm lucky to have such a wonderful family and such nice friends. It if wasn't for all of that, maybe I wouldn't have been able to throw every ounce of myself into my career for so many years. But now . . ." She sighed as they left the piazza and entered the narrow, shadowed streets leading to the church. "I'm getting older, Roe. I'm in my thirties now, you know. I'm tired of everyone baby-sitting me, telling me what to do, making decisions for me, treating me like a child. Vince says I'm a genius, but he doesn't treat me like one."

She looked guiltily at him a moment later. "I'm sorry. I didn't mean to sound disloyal or criticize your brother."

He glanced at her, wondering if this resentment explained her lack of concern about Vince's failing health.

"It's just that . . ." She waved her hand helplessly, as if trying to find a way to express her growing dissatisfaction. "Maybe I needed those tight reins when I was younger, but now . . . I feel like I'm strangling sometimes. And if I strangle, what will happen to my music? My work has always been the most important thing in my life, but now I think my life may wind up choking it, making it bland and pointless." She made a little sound of frustration. "Does that make any sense?"

He considered this seriously. Finally he said, "I don't know, Gingie. I've lived around creative people most of my life, and the insanity of it drove me far, far away. But . . . I understand needing to break free."

"Hey, are you two coming?" Milo's impatient voice echoed through the old stone street. Gingie called back as she and Roe picked up their pace. A moment later they entered the small, ancient, crumbling Piazza Santa Cecilia.

"The church dates back to the twelfth century," Roe explained as they approached it. "Most of it was refurbished in the seventeenth century, though one original mosaic still remains on the eastern wall. Wait, Gingie." He stopped her before she could enter the scarred wooden door. "Milo, give her your coat. A woman can't go into church in Italy with bare shoulders, Gingie."

She stared at him. "Women's shoulders are indecent? Camilla would be furious."

"Who's Camilla?" Roe asked, slipping the shiny trench coat over her soft, pale shoulders.

"Gingie's oldest sister," Milo supplied. "I dated her for a while when we were all a lot younger."

"That's how Milo and I met, actually," Gingie said, rolling up the cuffs of the coat. Roe was amazed. She even made that battered, oversized garment look like it was custom-made for her.

"Camilla's a radical socialist, a militant feminist, and a rather unforgiving activist," Milo explained.

"I take it things didn't work out between you?" Roe asked dryly.

"Well, the sex was great," Milo admitted, "but everything else was a dead loss."

"Milo, please," Gingie chided. "That's my sister you're talking about."

Feeling somewhat dazed, Roe followed them all into the church. There were a couple of worshippers inside. The priest nodded to Roe, then went to sit in the confessional, closing the ancient latticed door behind him to await the truly penitent.

"It's falling apart," Milo said sadly.

The cracked walls, fading frescoes, scarred wood, and bad wiring were all evidence that Santa Cecilia had seen better days.

"My mother had the roof repaired when I was a boy so that people would at least be safe in here," Roe said.

"Why is it in such terrible condition?" Gingie whispered.

Roe shrugged. "No money."

"But don't they collect money every Sunday?" Gingie asked.

"This isn't a wealthy island, Gingie. In order to restore the church, inside and out, it would take a lot more money than the people of Sontara can offer."

"So it just keeps going to ruin," Gingie said sadly.

"It's an old story in Italy," Roe told her.

Sandy and Milo quite naturally gravitated toward the organ. Roe followed Gingie over to a faded fresco on the northern wall.

"Is Saint Cecilia in this picture?" she asked.

"She's the girl about to be beheaded." He traced the outline for her.

She squinted at it, then recoiled when she finally made out the shape of the original painting. "It's so violent!"

"Santa Cecilia's story was pretty violent," Roe said. "She was a young Christian patrician in third-century Rome, betrothed, they say, to a pagan called Valerian. She had already pledged her virginity to God, however, and refused to consummate her marriage. Her husband, apparently taking it like a good sport, converted to Christianity."

"But they didn't live happily ever after?"

"No. Saints hardly ever lived happily ever after, Gingie. Valerian was arrested and executed, along with Cecilia's brother. Cecilia was arrested shortly after burying them. She was sentenced to be suffocated, and when that failed, she was beheaded."

"I hope it was a quick death," Gingie said softly.

"Unfortunately, it wasn't. Personally, I suspect there's no such thing as a painless death, but Cecilia's was particularly awful. The executioner's blow to her neck failed to kill her completely, and she lingered for three days in horrible agony."

"Oh, how terrible!"

"Her tomb was opened around the end of the sixteenth century. Her body, the story says, was well-preserved, but it quickly disintegrated through contact with the air. The sculptor Maderna made a life-size marble statue of the body, with her hands positioned like this," he showed her, "to represent the Holy Trinity."

"Have you seen the statue?"

He shook his head. "I've seen a good replica of it in the catacombs under Rome."

"That's such a sad story, Roe."

"Saints' lives are usually pretty grim," he agreed. He looked at the faded, dirty fresco. Even through years of grime and damage, he could make out the stark terror in Cecilia's posture and the violent swing of her executioner's blow. She was preserved here forever, always trapped in that vivid, terrifying second before the blade struck her neck. "Do you realize that man is the only creature on earth willing to die for an idea?" he mused.

Gingie took his arm. "I never thought of it that way before." She gazed at the fresco again. "She died very young, didn't she?"

"Probably," Roe said. "Actually, I should tell you that that story is a legend invented about two hundred years after Cecilia's death. It might not even be true."

After a thoughtful moment, Gingie said, "Maybe the real story is even worse."

"Maybe," he conceded.

"Patron saint of musicians," Gingie murmured thoughtfully.

She taxed him with questions about the village, the island, and their neighbors all through dinner, coming back often to the subject of the church. Weren't people upset about its being in such terrible condition? How much money would it take to restore it? How long would it take? He guessed as well as he could, the restoration of churches being a subject on which he could claim no expertise.

Gingie, apparently serious about this new leaf she was turning over, insisted on paying the bill. Looking past her two lovers, she met Roe's eyes and said, "Shall we go home?"

As he gazed into those lush blue eyes, fringed by thick lashes and framed by her pale face and blond hair, he felt a surge of something painful. Sharing her with anyone, even for a moment, was suddenly a sacrifice.

Apparently oblivious to Roe, Sandy got in his way and followed Gingie outside, trailing at her heels like an adoring pet. Milo launched into an obscure argument with Gingie about the name of some restaurant in Little Italy.

Roe hesitated, wondering if he was really going to throw Gingie out of the villa as soon as he spoke to Vince again. Then, with a feeling of helplessness, he followed her out of the restaurant and into the gentle night.

Five

*A*fter leaving Signora Gambarossa's *trattoria,* they gave Zu Aspanu's donkey a drink of water and then began leading it home. Since it was dark, Roe decided they had better take the long way, sticking to the coastal road, rather than using the shortcut they had taken upon Gingie's arrival. As they walked through the tranquillity of a quiet country evening, Sandy surprised Roe by uttering his first sentence in over three hours.

"What do you do, Roe?"

"I work for a travel company."

"Do you mean you're a travel agent?" Gingie said in surprise.

"No, I'm an expedition guide for an adventure travel company. You know, wilderness treks, safaris, that kind of thing. I take small groups of people, ten to twenty at a time, around Africa."

"It's a big continent," Milo said from the other side of the donkey. "Where in Africa?"

"All over, really. I've been doing it for fourteen years."

"You must have started very young," Gingie said. "How did you wind up in a job like that? It's a long way from Hollywood."

"That was the main attraction," he admitted dryly. "It started when I was twenty. I went on one of the company's treks, a hiking trip into the Virunga Mountains to see gorillas in their natural habitat."

"You didn't need to go that far, Roe," Milo said. "You could have just come to the first club Gingie and I ever played together."

"How long did your trip last?" Gingie asked, ignoring Milo.

"Four weeks. And I loved it. So when we got back to Nairobi, I cashed in my ticket back to the States and talked the company into hiring me on as camp master for the gorilla trips."

"Camp master? What does that mean?" Gingie prodded.

He grinned. "Drudgery, mostly. I was in charge of acquiring all our food and water on the road and of keeping all the supplies well-stocked and in order. I got people to make camp at the end of the day and to strike camp in the morning. I organized all the meals — who had to cook each evening, what we ate, who cleaned up, who collected firewood. Stuff like that."

"Sounds rather like a rock band's manager, except for the firewood," Milo commented. "How long did you do this glamorous work?"

"For about a year. Then I took some time off and got licensed to drive and repair their vehicles, learned some first aid, improved my Swahili, got additional training. Then they made me an expedition co-leader and; after a few more years, an expedition leader."

"But not just in the Virungas?"

"No. After the first year, I started moving into other territories. I learned Kenya, Tanzania, Botswana, and Zimbabwe. I eventually took over the Nairobi to Johannesburg run. That usually took anywhere from fifteen to twenty weeks, depending on how we did it. Obviously, we didn't hike it," he added. "We traveled in an allpurpose four-wheel drive camper truck, specially designed for the company."

"Twenty weeks in the bush?" Milo said in horror.

"Well, not entirely," Roe said. "We also visited cities and villages on the way. We probably slept indoors once a week."

"How did you shower?" Milo demanded.

"There's a shower apparatus on the side of every truck." Roe grinned when Milo grunted doubtfully. "I got used to it: '

"If you've lived that way for fourteen years, I guess so."

"Oh, but surely you aren't always on the road?" Gingie asked.

"No. I get vacations. And I've occasionally been posted in cities — Cairo, Nairobi, Marrakech — for long stretches."

"Why is that?"

"It depends." He caught the donkey's bridle as the animal stumbled slightly, then continued, "I worked in the office in Marrakech for a few months to help the new operations director learn the ropes. I had learned how to run operations in Nairobi, after I first caught malaria and the company didn't want me going right back out on the road. Then they assigned me to the Cairo office after the time I got banged up in Botswana, and —"

"You got hurt?" Gingie interrupted, sounding as if she thought he might still be in pain. "How?"

"It's kind of embarrassing," Roe said sheepishly.

"I love embarrassing stories," Milo said with relish. "Come on, tell us."

"Well . . . We were at a fairly civilized campsite in the Okavango Delta," Roe began.

"Define civilized," Milo instructed.

"It had a latrine."

"My, my, is no place safe from technology?" Milo murmured.

"And I made the mistake of using the latrine in the middle of the night."

"That was a mistake?" Gingie repeated. "But lots of people . . . you know."

"In the bush, it's a mistake," Roe assured her.

"Don't you know there are lions and tigers and bears out there?" Milo added.

"Oh, really, Milo," Gingie said.

"He's not entirely wrong," Roe said. "We were in one of the most remote regions of the world, and I had carefully instructed all my clients not to leave their tents after dark. Plenty of tourists, thinking they're in a zoo instead of the bush, get attacked in camp on their way to latrines or showers at night, so I always make sure my clients stay inside. Tough guy that I am though, I had contracted a mild form of dysentery, and I decided that I definitely couldn't wait until morning."

"You were attacked by something on the way to the latrine?" Gingie was shocked. "It sounds worse than Manhattan!"

He grinned. "No, I was very careful on my way there. But when I was ready to go back to my tent, there was a hippopotamus waiting for me right outside the latrine."

"Oh, but they're so cute," Gingie said.

"They also kill more tourists than any other animal in Africa."

"No! Really?"

"But why?" Milo asked.

"They don't actually hang out hoping to kill people," Roe explained, "but they panic if you get between them and the water. Well, we were on a tiny island right in the middle of a swamp. He kept his eyes on me, so no matter which way I moved, I was between him and the water."

"So he trampled you outside the latrine?" Milo asked, his face scrunched up in an apparent effort to form a mental picture.

"Not exactly. I ducked back inside the latrine, which was made of some flimsy thatched stuff. He went berserk and tore it down around my ears. *Then* he trampled me."

"You were trampled inside a latrine by a hippopotamus in a swamp in the middle of the night," Gingie said, as if expecting him to deny it. When he didn't, she said, "That sounds so . . ."

"Undignified?" Roe supplied helpfully.

"I'd have said exotic," Milo said generously.

"*Dangerous* is the word I was looking for," Gingie said at last. "You must have been pretty badly hurt."

"I was," Roe admitted. "What the hippo didn't do to me, the hospital in Gaborone and the trip back to Nairobi did."

"When did all this happen?" Milo asked.

"About eight years ago."

"And you didn't quit your job?" Milo asked incredulously.

"No." Roe shrugged. "I still wanted to be there."

"Talk about occupational hazards," Gingie said.

"And I thought *I* had played some real dives," Milo mused.

"I guess you couldn't lead expeditions into the bush if you were all broken into pieces," Gingie said.

"No. My company needed somebody to run the operations center in Cairo at the time, so I spent almost a year living and working there. But then I was ready to go back on the road, so I took over the Morocco and West African run. I did that for two years, then I partnered an old hand on the Egypt and Sudan route for another year. At that point, I started doing the trans-Africa run. That takes six to nine months per trip, depending —"

"Depending on which way you go," Milo said. "Gee, Roe, I hadn't realized what a masochist you were."

Roe glanced at Gingie and thought, *That must be my problem.* Aloud, he said casually, "The life-style suits me."

"Living in the bush?" Milo asked disbelievingly. "Out of touch for months at a time? Waking up every morning in the middle of nowhere, hundreds, perhaps thousands of miles away from the nearest margarita?"

"He doesn't drink," Gingie chided.

"A five-week drive in any direction from a decent jazz club," Milo continued.

"I'm sure the local people have good music," Gingie said.

"Not a decent sushi bar as far as the eye can see!"

"Not everybody likes raw fish, Milo."

"And women — how can you go so long without women, Roe?"

"About half my clients are women," Roe responded.

"And *they're* a thousand miles from the nearest hairdresser," Milo said dismissively. "I can just imagine the appeal of curling up next to a woman who's been fending off crazed hippopotamuses all day. Hippopotami?"

"Women have their appeal in any circumstances, Milo," Roe said with a reminiscent smile.

"They do?" Gingie said hesitantly.

"Roe! You *hound*, you!" Milo nudged Gingie delightedly. "At least he's not totally devoid of normal vices."

"You sleep with your clients?" Gingie asked, unaccountably disturbed by this information.

"Well . . ." Roe noticed her tone and wished he would have stopped talking ten minutes ago. He didn't often talk about himself. *Serves me right for relaxing so much around her.*

"Doesn't the company have rules about that?" Gingie prodded.

"Oh, Gingie, you're so naïve," Milo said sadly.

"Well?" she persisted.

"Discretion is one of my most highly developed skills," Roe replied at last.

"Oh." After an awkward silence, Gingie added, "I see."

"That's your celebrity upbringing shining through, Roe," Milo said. "If only all of us could learn to be so discreet, Gingie."

"I'm discreet," Gingie protested.

Roe listened to them bicker, relieved that Milo had distracted her from the subject of his sexual adventures. It was none of her business anyhow, and he had nothing to be ashamed of — especially not with both of her lovers preparing to bed down with her on Sontara — but he nevertheless had a strange feeling that he didn't want her to hear about the women he'd known. Maybe it was because she had sounded absurdly dismayed by the realization that he had a private life, too. He tried to shrug off his confusion.

"Discreet?" Milo scoffed. "My dear girl, dumping an entire plate of spaghetti and tomato sauce over the head of the president of our esteemed ex-record company was not an act of discretion."

"That was different," Gingie explained reasonably.

"Why did you do it?" Roe asked, reluctantly curious.

"He was rude." Her tone implied that should be obvious.

"How rude?" Roe persisted. Gingie seemed to be the kind of woman who would only resort to such tactics in extreme circumstances.

"He insulted me, and he embarrassed Sandy. He was just like the creep who signed us to our first recording contract."

"Four ex-companies ago," Milo added for Roe's benefit.

"They all think they own you, or own your talent. This guy thought I was obliged to favor him with my, um, attentions," Gingie said furiously. "I explained to him why that was absolutely out of the question. I even gave him a copy of Camilla's doctoral thesis on the subject."

"I'm sure that helped enormously," Roe said dryly.

"It's a little long-winded," Gingie admitted, "but it gets the point across about the bondage of women through the centuries due to misappropriation of sexual favors."

"Gingie's family is very intellectual," Milo explained.

"I see," Roe said, still pretty confused.

"Well, he confronted me at some party or other, and I was tired of brushing him off tactfully. He was drunk, and things just got out of hand. I *wish* Vince wouldn't make me go to those things in the first place. Sandy, don't you remember what happened that night you and I went to that one company's promotional party with Luke Swain, before he married Nina?"

Sandy nodded, and Milo told Roe, "That was when Gingie alienated our third label. Vince thought Luke — another rock star — could keep Gingie under control for an evening." Milo sighed. "He should have known better."

"Luke was busy falling in love at the time," Gingie said understandingly. "Anyhow, I'm tired of Vince assigning people to baby-sit me!"

Like me, Roe thought, feeling absurdly guilty. Gingie apparently didn't realize he was just another baby-sitter. "Maybe you really *shouldn't* go to these parties," he said.

"Tell that to your brother," Gingie said huffily. "I've tried, but he doesn't have any respect for my opinion."

There was another awkward silence. Roe tried to sort out his jumbled impulses. Though loyal to his brother, he knew that Vince seldom heeded anyone else's opinion, least of all a woman's. Vince undoubtedly pushed Gingie into public appearances she didn't want to make, then chastised her when things didn't go well. And since Vince was a perfectionist, nothing could ever go well enough to suit him. Roe himself had fought Vince's influence often enough to sympathize with Gingie's evident frustration.

However, although Roe knew none of the details, he was aware that Vince had discovered Gingie when she was playing badly paid gigs in the kind of dives Milo had hinted at, and he had guided her steady rise to international stardom. Vince also had his reasons for being so compulsive, Roe remembered with a twinge of pain. If Vince only knew of one way to deal with Gingie, Roe could at least forgive him for it.

In any event, Roe resented Gingie's criticism of his brother only a day before he was due to undergo major surgery. Had she expressed concern about Vince even once since her arrival? he fumed. Roe's anger toward her became even easier to fuel as they finally reached the villa and he had to figure out how to tactfully handle the sleeping arrangements.

This woman was bad news. If he reminded himself of that often enough, he might remember not to become so fond of her. He might remember not to think about those innocent blue eyes, that honey-rich voice, and those long, long legs. At least there would be no more watching her bedroom window at night with desire pulsing through his body. God alone knew what would go on in that room tonight. Roe was positive *he* didn't want to know.

It was that firm realization that made him decide that discretion was definitely the better part of valor. As soon as they had unloaded the donkey cart, Roe said casually to the two men, "Gingie knows where everything is. She'll make sure you're comfortable. I'm going to return Zu Aspanu's donkey to him."

"Tonight?" Gingie said uncertainly. "But it's so late."

"He needs it first thing in the morning, Gingie."

She took his hand. He tried to shake her off without being too obvious about it. He was *not* going to become part of her entourage. "I'll come with you," she said.

"That's not necessary, Gingie."

"But it's such a steep, rocky path, and it's so dark out," she protested.

"I'll take the road. I'll be perfectly safe."

"Well, at least take a flashlight."

"I know the way. I don't need one."

"But, Roe!"

"Don't worry, I'll be fine," he said impatiently. He wasn't used to being fussed over like this.

"I'll wait up for you," she offered.

Unable to stop himself, Roe looked incredulously from Gingie to Milo and Sandy, then back again. "Don't bother. I'll see you in the morning."

As she watched him lead the donkey into the night, Gingie fretted in the shadowy light of the front door to Roe's villa.

"I shouldn't have criticized his brother," she said unhappily to Milo. "I think Roe's mad at me."

"Well, I wouldn't do it again, Gingie," Milo advised blandly. "At least not for a few days."

"A few days?" She looked at Milo, unable to see his eyes behind his rose-colored glasses. "Why do you say that?"

"We'll talk about it later. Why don't you show me my room? I can't remember the last time I slept."

After another longing glance into the shadows that had swallowed up Roe, Gingie said, "Okay."

"I wish I had known the house was perched on a cliff," Milo said. "I never would have agreed to this. I hate heights."

"There's a bedroom that faces the road instead of the sea," Gingie told Milo.

Sandy picked up his two guitars, indicating he was ready to go inside.

"I suppose I'll have to carry my own keyboard," Milo said in disgust. He grunted as he heaved it into his arms. "What's the point of being famous if you still have to do manual labor?"

"Come on, I'll show you your rooms," Gingie said on a sigh. Somehow the whole evening seemed anticlimactic now that Roe was gone.

*T*here was hell to pay when Roe rode his bicycle into the village the following morning to buy more groceries and find out why Maria Sellerio hadn't come to clean the house and cook lunch.

Signora Gambarossa, who probably hadn't intended any real harm, had interrogated Gingie between courses in her *trattoria* the night before, and she had already gossiped to half the people on Sontara by nine o'clock the next morning. Everyone knew that the two bachelors staying in the villa with Gingie bore no blood relationship to her. And thanks to Roe's cousin Gaspare and his passion for American pop culture, everyone quickly learned that these same two men were reputed to be Gingie's lovers. Within just a few hours, the scandal surrounding Gingie was as severe as the volcano of gossip that had erupted over Don Ciccio's golf cart.

"Certe cose non si fanno," Signor Sellerio's mother-in-law explained haughtily to Roe in the bread shop. *Some things simply aren't done.*

Don Ciccio was concerned that those wicked rock musicians from New York were taking advantage of Gingie, who was such a nice girl, after all. What was Roe doing to protect her honor?

Signor Sellerio demanded a thorough explanation of the whole situation from Roe, insisting he wouldn't let his daughter Maria return to Roe's house unless he was satisfied that nothing immoral was going on. Unspeakably depressed by the thought of losing Maria's domestic skills, Roe lied shamelessly, assuring Signor Sellerio that he had everything under control. He secretly hoped that Maria wouldn't inadvertently see something shocking and report it back to her father; Roe's life wouldn't be worth a counterfeit nickel in that case.

He found his young cousin Gaspare chatting up girls in the main piazza. Resisting the urge to turn him over his knee, Roe told Gaspare that if he wanted to live until his eighteenth birthday, he'd better repair the damage he had done around town with his careless tongue that morning.

Roe was on his way home when he encountered Zu Aspanu, who was headed into town with his donkey cart. Zu Aspanu listened to an account of Roe's rotten morning and said, *"E chi n'hammu a vidiri li spicchia?"*

It was an old Sicilian proverb which Roe was pretty sure meant: It's better not to look too closely into these matters. As usual, his uncle's advice was the most sensible.

He decided not to go home for the main midday meal. He could let three full-grown world travelers fend for themselves for one meal, Signor Sellerio having agreed to send Maria to Roe's house again the following morning. Accepting his uncle's invitation, Roe sat under an ancient, gnarled tree with the old man, shared a simple meal of bread, cheese, and olives, and rested quietly in the shade for an hour.

This is what it used to be like on Sontara, Roe thought nostalgically as a fly buzzed lazily in the afternoon sun. The leaves rustled softly overhead, the donkey munched on its grain, Zu Aspanu snored in the shadows, and the church bell at Santa Cecilia chimed twice in the distance. Before Gingie, the days on Sontara had had a predictable pattern, a rhythm as old as the olive trees that clung to the rocky hills.

Gingie had changed everything. Roe had come here to rest, and now he was trying to suppress a scandal. He wanted to be numb, and he was feeling angry, amused, lustful, or moonstruck every time he turned around. He needed a quiet place to lick his wounds, and she was inflicting new ones. He . . .

"Porca miseria!" Uttering his uncle's favorite curse, Roe sat bolt upright. *Lisa.* He hadn't thought about his little sister in ages. At least not since early yesterday morning. How could the antics of one blond singer make him so thoughtless?

"Cosa?" Zu Aspanu grumbled. *"Ma che fai?"*

"Sorry, I've got to go," Roe apologized in his garbled Italian. "I must call the clinic to see how my sister is."

"The phones are working again?" his uncle asked absently.

Roe nodded. "Since yesterday. *Ciao.*"

He bicycled home as fast as he could, so he was flushed and perspiring when he arrived. A brief investigation proved that the house was empty. He found Milo on the terrace, sitting with his back to the view. The blond musician was playing a complex game of solitaire with two decks of cards, having shoved numerous lunch dishes out of his way.

"Gingie forced me to come out here," Milo said grumpily. "She's under the delusion that fresh air would be good for me."

"Where is she?" Roe asked before he could stop himself.

Milo gestured over his shoulder. Looking into the distance, Roe saw Gingie and Sandy on the beach. "She tried to make him go jogging with her this morning, but he resisted," Milo explained. "I guess he decided she'd feel rejected if he also refused a power walk this afternoon."

Sure enough, Sandy was trailing meekly behind Gingie as her long legs carried her swiftly across the sand. As if alerted to Roe's presence by some sixth sense, Gingie stopped for a moment and looked up toward the villa, one hand anchoring her broad-brimmed hat to her head. Spotting him as he leaned over the balcony, she waved to Roe. Wishing he didn't enjoy this first glimpse of her today quite so much, he waved back.

"I noticed she exercises a lot," Roe murmured. Feigning sleep, he had surreptitiously watched her slim, limber body for the past few days while she jogged, swam, did her sit-ups, or worked out on the beach.

"Yeah, she exercises a lot," Milo agreed gloomily. "And she refuses to respect my Constitutional right not to."

Suppressing a smile, Roe surveyed the mess of dirty dishes and leftover food on the table before Milo. "I found out why Maria didn't come this morning." Not wishing to elaborate, he concluded, "I've taken care of it. She'll be back tomorrow."

"Don't worry about this." His expression hidden by his rose-colored glasses, Milo gestured to the dirty dishes and the remains of what appeared to be a gourmet meal. "I told Gingie that since I had to cook it, she has to clean it up. She agreed."

"Looks like you're a good cook," Roe said, glancing into the serving bowl.

"I've become one during the past year. After I moved in with Gingie, it became a matter of self-preservation. Have you ever tasted her cooking?"

Stone-faced, Roe shook his head.

"You're a lucky man, then. And her sister," Milo added, "is even worse."

"Camilla?"

"Letitia."

"You know the whole family?" Roe asked carefully.

Milo nodded absently as he made a few moves in his solitaire game. "Yeah, I know them all. Even her father, who's kind of an intellectual version of Sandy. Mind you, I figure Professor Potter was just smart enough to stop trying to get a word in edgewise in that family about thirty years ago."

Uncomfortable about the interest he felt for the woman Milo lived with, Roe nevertheless asked, "Her father is a professor?"

Milo sighed in defeat and started scooping his cards off the table. "A professor of anthropology. He teaches at Ann Arbor. Gingie's mother is a professor of women's studies. Gingie herself is reputed to be the stupid one in her family, though I think that's a fallacy. Have you ever tried arguing with her? She possesses a talent for empirical reasoning unlike anyone I've ever known."

Roe nodded as he glanced down at the beach again. Gingie was racing toward the stone stairs carved into the cliff. Sandy followed diffidently. "I know what you mean. Everything she says sounds so nonsensical, but then you gradually find yourself agreeing with her."

"Precisely," Milo said, shuffling his cards. "Quite apart from that, she has an uncanny knack for dealing with people. Except for record-company executives, I mean. Gingie gets whatever she wants. Not because she's famous, not because she's talented, not even because she's persistent. People just wind up wanting to do whatever they can for her."

Roe plopped into a chair, frowning as he thought this over. "Why do you suppose that is?" he wondered aloud.

Milo shrugged. "Maybe it's because she's the nicest person in the whole world." For once, there was no sarcasm or dryness in his tone. Roe realized he was quite serious. "Wanna play a hand of gin rummy?"

"I . . . No, thanks, Milo. I've got to make a phone call."

"You're back!" Gingie cried breathlessly, reaching the terrace. Behind her, Sandy waved to Roe in silent greeting. Gingie asked, "Are you hungry?"

"No. I'm going inside to make a call." Roe rose abruptly and left Gingie staring after him. He disliked being rude to her, but not nearly as much as he disliked the way looking at her flushed, eager face and sparkling blue eyes made him feel. He wanted to hug her to him, kiss her soft mouth in greeting, run his palms down her slim, straight back. He wanted to soak up all the effervescent joy that bubbled out of her.

Milo was right. Gingie had a strong effect on people. No wonder she was so successful. How could a person not feel good around her?

But he didn't, he realized. Not right now, at least. He felt something as sharp as pain, and it angered him. It made him feel uncomfortable, embarrassed, even ashamed to realize that he was jealous. He couldn't believe this was happening to him. To *him.* After all, there wasn't anyone in the world who knew better than Roe Hunter not to get mixed up with celebrities, because he knew that there wasn't any creature in the world as unstable, needy, narcissistic, self-absorbed, and careless as a celebrity.

Gingie had already turned his peaceful little island into a caldron of gossip. She was carrying on with not one but *two* men right under Roe's roof, even after he had explained to her how traditional the life-style and values were on Sontara. She had even touched him and looked at him with open invitation yesterday as they rode into town to meet both of her lovers.

How could he still be taken in by a little charm, vulnerability, and friendliness on her part? She didn't even care that the man who had managed her life and career for nearly ten years was undergoing major surgery today.

Having worked himself into a fine temper, Roe went to the study and telephoned the clinic in California. His sister came to the phone, but upon realizing it was he who was calling, she snarled that she was only staying in that crummy joint because of the way he had *threatened* her in LA.

"And *don't* bother calling again, Roe, because I don't want to talk to you! I hate you! You don't care about me, you're just calling to relieve your mealy-mouthed conscience!"

"Lisa, I love —" He heard her slam the phone down with venomous force. Roe closed his eyes and hung up. He swallowed hard. He had known it would be like this, he reminded himself patiently. He had known she wouldn't thank him for sending her there. He'd been warned it would take a while for her to come to terms with her addiction and stop lashing out at him.

He had known, but it didn't hurt any less. "Please, Lisa," he whispered. "I couldn't let you just . . . I just couldn't." As rigidly as he had trained himself not to interfere in other people's lives, sometimes interfering was the only way.

He and Vince were two sides of a coin, he acknowledged. Vince had tried to take control of everything, and Roe had tried to save himself by refusing to take control. Vince was learning, at the cost of his health, that he couldn't control everyone and everything, just as Roe had learned, in a bitter and painful lesson, that sometimes you had to step in, no matter how much you didn't want to. This was one of those times. Ironically, he supposed that his mother, wherever she was, had long since forgiven him for not stepping in ten years ago, whereas Lisa seemed as if she might never forgive him for stepping in at last.

"Roe?" Gingie wandered into the study, looking sunny and bright, long-legged and lovely in her little dress of seacolored cotton that had dozens of silky tassels hanging from it. "Oh, you're off the phone!"

"What do you want, Gingie?" he asked quietly.

"I was just thinking, why don't we all go out tonight? Is there someplace on the island with good music? Maybe we —"

"How could you possibly think I'd want to go out with you tonight?" he exploded.

Her jaw dropped, and her beautiful blue eyes went saucer-wide. She put a hand up to her chest, obviously shocked by his outburst. "I . . . I . . ." She blinked. "I'm sorry. I just thought . . ."

"No, you didn't think, Gingie." Everything hurt. Everything came crashing down on him, and without forethought, he found himself lashing out at her. "You *never* think, do you?"

"I know you said you wanted to be left . . ." She swallowed. "I'm sorry. I just thought you liked me. Us. Me."

"I might have," he said through gritted teeth, "if you had shown even a *little* consideration."

"Are you mad because my friends came?" she asked despairingly.

Her eyes misted up. It made him feel guilty, which made him even madder. "Do you know where I've been this morning, Gingie?"

"The village?" she answered tentatively.

"Do you know what I've been doing there?" When she shook her head, he pulled a wooden chair away from his mother's elegant walnut desk and indicated that Gingie should sit in it. She did so, crossing her legs. The action drew his gaze to her milky smooth thighs, and the thoughts they provoked made his temper catch fire.

"I spent the entire morning trying to dampen all the rumors about what's going on out here," he began accusingly.

She met his gaze steadily. "There are always rumors about me," she admitted. "I've learned to ignore them."

"Yes, I've realized that. But did it occur to you that they're affecting me?" he snapped.

"It's best if you ignore them, too," she assured him.

"Damn it, Gingie, I live here!"

"I thought you lived in Africa," she said in confusion.

"I live here, too." He was *not* going to let her turn this into another one of those bizarre circular conversations. "And I've spent the entire morning lying through my teeth, assuring all my neighbors and relatives that nothing immoral is going on out here."

She looked puzzled. *"Is* something immoral going on here?"

He let his breath out in a rush. "Look, if you've got to have two men in bed instead of one, that's your business. And if the gossip in the tabloids doesn't bother you, more power to you. But on an island where an affianced couple isn't even allowed to live together before they get married, who the hell do you think you are to come here and wave both your boyfriends under everybody's noses?"

"Oh, my God," Gingie said slowly. "They all think . . ." She shook her head. "But I thought that I'd at least be safe from that, this far off the beaten path."

"You should have thought of that before Milo and Sandy moved into your room."

"But they didn't! They've got their own rooms!"

"Big deal."

"You don't understand," she insisted.

"What I understand," he said tersely, "is that you are totally self-centered and thoughtless. You don't give a damn that you've offended everyone on this island, you don't give a damn that you've disrupted my life —"

"I didn't mean —"

"And you've made it absolutely clear that you don't give a damn about Vince, after everything he's done for you."

She shot out of her chair. "I *do* care about Vince. You've got it wrong! I'm sorry I said what I did last night. I just —"

"If you care so much, how can you suggest that we go out and party tonight, when we should be sitting here by the phone waiting to hear if he pulled through the surgery all right?" Roe demanded furiously.

Gingie looked as if he had slapped her. "What did you say?"

"You wouldn't give Vince any peace and quiet," he continued mercilessly, "so he had to send you halfway around the world just to have his operation. God knows *I* didn't want to be your baby-sitter, but where the hell else could he send you? I'm beginning to fully understand why he couldn't trust you to run your own life while he was laid up."

"He what?" Gingie's voice was strangled and breathless. Her wide-eyed expression was distressed and shocked.

Afraid he might be laying it on too thick, but somehow unable to stop himself now that he had started, Roe added, "And all you can think about is having fun on your *vacation.*"

Gingie started gulping in air like a drowning person. She squeezed her eyes shut and mumbled, "A vacation. That's what he said. He wanted me to get away, relax, be on my own. I was supposed to . . ." A tear rolled down her cheek, shocking Roe. "I thought he trusted me."

"Gingie . . ." Roe's anger started draining away as fast as it had come. Her tears made his insides crumble. He would prefer it if she hit him, rather than cry because of something he said. "Gingie, I'm —"

"He's having an operation today?" she asked suddenly. She opened her eyes again and looked fiercely at Roe, wringing her hands and crying. "Did you say he's having an *operation?*"

"Oh, Christ, Gingie." Roe sank wearily into the chair she had just vacated and stared at the floor, finally realizing just how much Vince was sheltering Gingie from reality. "He didn't tell you, did he?"

Six

Gingie sat on the couch; so distressed by Roe's news that she actually felt numb.

Heart trouble. Surgery. Convalescence.

Roe's words echoed inside her head. He paused here and there in his explanation to ask if she had heard him, if she understood everything he was saying. She nodded, staring blankly at the floor, feeling drained and stupid with surprise.

After Roe had finished explaining the procedure Vince had to undergo, there was a long silence. Finally, he said, "Gingie, you're white as death. Can I get you something? Some espresso with sugar in it?"

She shook her head. When he persisted, she said, "No!" It came out sharper than she had intended, so she immediately said, "Sorry."

Perhaps sensing how cold she was, Roe sat next to her on the worn couch and took her hand. His palm was warm, hard, and full of strength. She clutched it.

"He never told me," she said dully. "I know he works very hard. My career is very complicated. He used to manage two other groups, but he cut them out a couple of years ago. I thought it was because he was making enough money, or maybe because he wanted to take it easy." She sighed. "I guess it was because his health was forcing him to cut back."

He squeezed her hand. She suddenly cried, "Oh, Roe, why didn't he tell me?"

"I guess he didn't want you to worry, Gingie." He brushed her fluffy hair away from her eyes with gentle fingers.

"I have a right to worry!" she said fiercely. "I've known Vince since I was twenty-two. How could he just not tell me?"

"Vince needs to feel in control, even when he's flat on his back and under anesthesia," Roe explained. "I guess he wanted to pretend for your sake that everything was normal."

"He just didn't trust me." She was wounded by that realization. "We had another fight after . . . after I dumped a plate of spaghetti over that guy's head at that party. I told Vince I was tired of him trying to keep me in a cage, watching my every move more closely than a mother. So a week later, he said, 'Gingie, why don't you get away for a while? Do something on your own?'"

"He meant coming here?"

She nodded. "I've never done anything all by myself before, so we talked about it and agreed this would be a good compromise. He said I'd be comfortable in the villa and he could make sure there was someone to take care of it for me." She pulled Roe's hand onto her lap and stroked it absently, comforted by the physical contact. "I thought it was his way of letting me spread my wings a little. I thought maybe he was ready to stop . . ." She sighed tearfully. "Oh, Roe, I just had to get away from the whole thing, and I thought he understood at last. Is it so difficult?"

"No." His touch was warm. "*I* understand, Gingie."

"Do you?" She turned to look at him, losing herself in the glittering golden depths of his eyes.

"Sure. Why do you think I've been hiding in the bush for fourteen years?"

"I thought you liked it."

"I do," he admitted. "But I went there to get away from my parents, my stepmother, my sister, my brother, and everything that went with them. I guess," he added slowly. "I went there to get away from myself, too."

"And did you?"

He grinned, his smile looking so boyish against the dark masculinity of his features. "Not exactly. But through trial and error, I became someone that I liked living with."

"That's why I needed to leave for a while. I've put all my eggs in one basket, Roe. My whole life has been about my work. That's okay. I don't regret it. I mean, I wouldn't be where I am if I hadn't made that sacrifice. It didn't even seem like a sacrifice. Until recently."

"And now?"

She folded her long legs underneath her and shifted closer to him. His body was warm. She stifled the urge to snuggle up against him. "I know I'll never be normal," she began pensively.

He laced his fingers with hers. "You mean you'll never be ordinary," he corrected.

She smiled. "I guess that sounds better." She studied their entwined hands, enjoying the contrast of his dark golden skin against the pearly paleness of her own. He had a faint scar running across his knuckles. She traced it as she said, "But I need to change and grow just like other people. And I felt stifled back in New York."

"Vince doesn't let you do anything for yourself." It was not a question.

"I don't want to sound like I'm blaming him, Roe. He has his reasons. I'm very good at what I do, but I'm not much good at anything else. My life was a mess when Vince met me. I signed the wrong contracts, misscheduled all my gigs, worked with the wrong people. I have no ability to handle money, either. I was so deep in debt that it took a platinum album to bail me out. But instead of teaching me how to handle these things, he and my accountant simply took over my life. They pay my bills and give me a weekly allowance. Do you believe that? I was named one of the ten most successful women in America *again* last year, and I don't even have a checkbook. I just sign whatever Vince and the accountant put in front of me."

"You're lucky Vince is so honest," Roe said.

"I know," she agreed. "I've heard all those horror stories about rock stars who've been left penniless by crooked managers."

"Oh, Gingie." Roe stroked her hair again. This time she turned toward him and rubbed her cheek against his palm. She felt affection and contentment when he touched her. She felt him filling places she had only recently begun to realize were empty. "You were just the fix Vince needed after my mother died."

"What do you mean?"

He traced her cheekbone with his forefinger, hypnotizing her with his touch. "It's old history," he said after a moment.

"Tell me," she pleaded. "I won't tell anyone else."

After a moment of indecision, he began, "My father split on us when

I was five and Vince was fifteen. My mom . . ." He shook his head. "I loved my mom, Gingie, and nobody could have made me feel more loved or cherished, but she had a lot of serious problems."

"I know she died of a drug overdose," Gingie said carefully.

"She pretty much fell apart after Vince's father died," Roe explained. "The studio wasn't willing to wait for her to get over his death before she finished her next picture, so they put her on uppers when it was time for work and downers when it was time for bed. That was the beginning of it. She got clean and sober for a while, then she met and married my father."

"The photos of the two of them together look like something from a fairy tale," Gingie said. She saw the flash of sorrow in his face and shifted closer. His hand drifted down to her neck, then he slid his arm around her shoulders. She gave in to her impulses at last and curled against him, wondering how she had waited four whole days to touch him like this.

"My father, even today, has absolutely no understanding of alcoholism. Thirty-five years ago he was at least as self-centered as he is now. He drank often, and he occasionally drank very heavily, but he kept it from affecting his work. So he couldn't understand why my mother couldn't stop once she got going. He was very . . . critical and contemptuous of her 'weakness.' They had a pretty stormy relationship. Vince remembers more than I do," he said quietly. "I'm lucky. I can remember the shouting, but not what they said to each other."

The pain of his memories filled the silence around them. After a moment, he continued, "Zu Aspanu left Hollywood and returned to Sicily shortly after I was born. He didn't enjoy Hollywood anymore, and he and my father couldn't stand each other. My mother . . . It was inevitable, I suppose, that she wound up getting into barbiturates again. When my father found out, he walked out on her. On all of us. They were divorced within a year. She dried out again, and Vince and I were able to stay with her."

"So Vince, at fifteen, found himself virtual head of the household," Gingie guessed. When Roe nodded, she added, "You know, he never talks to me about himself. Never."

"It's not his way," Roe said. It wasn't usually Roe's way, either, and he couldn't imagine why he suddenly wanted to tell this bizarre blond rock star all the gory details. Maybe it was because she looked as if she desperately wanted to understand. "Vince just took charge of everything, the way his father apparently had. He got Mom up in the mornings, sent her to work, made my lunch, packed me off to school, then went to school himself. He controlled all the money and kept her on an allowance. Not only did it keep us from going broke, it also meant she had no spare money for booze or pills. She had to account to him for every penny she spent, and he found out every time she got her hands on something dangerous."

"This sounds kind of familiar," Gingie said uneasily. Except for the dangerous substances, it sounded a little like her own relationship with Vince.

"He was just a kid," Roe muttered, absently caressing her bare shoulder. "It had to be hell for him. Ironically, though, it was his taking charge that accounted for the only stability in my childhood. I was ten before I started to realize that my sweet, generous mother was seriously self-destructive. That was when Vince was so busy with college that he started needing my help to keep an eye on Mom."

"But you were only a child," Gingie protested. "What could he ask you to do?"

"I started being the one to wake her up and get her off to work. It was a nightmare for both of us. She was one of the most talented, respected actresses in the world, being bossed around every morning by her ten-year-old son. By the time I was twelve, I didn't want to do it anymore. I hated taking drinks away from her, searching her purse, checking her wallet. Between Vince on one side and me on the other, it's no wonder she never married again. She had enough males trying to run her life.

"Then Vince and I started to fight, because I couldn't deal with her his way, and he couldn't deal with her any other way. The only peace and quiet the three of us ever had was when we were here. My mother was a different person on Sontara — calm, happy, secure. Every time we came here, I begged her to let us live here, I pleaded with her not to go back to Hollywood. But she was . . ." He shrugged. "I guess she was like you, in that respect. She had to work. She'd rather be dead than not work."

"But her life was killing her." Gingie was saddened.

"Vince got married to Alice and moved out, but he kept riding me to keep an eye on Mom. She fell off the wagon in the middle of making *Forgive Us Our Trespasses*, and Vince nearly killed me."

"Didn't she win an Oscar for that fihn?" Gingie asked.

"Yes. And a Cannes Film Festival Award. She was a lot more than just a beautiful woman."

"Yes," Gingie agreed, smoothing his sad frown with gentle fingers. He rubbed his forehead against her hand. Wanting to hear more about his youth, she stifled the urge to kiss him.

"Then Vince and Alice moved from LA to New York. After that, no matter how hard I tried, I couldn't control my mother."

"But you were a boy, Roe. And people can't be controlled if they want to destroy themselves, not every minute of the day."

He nodded. "It took me a long time to learn that. As soon as Vince was gone, my mother started drinking often and taking all kinds of pills. I'd get up for school in the morning and find her passed out on the bathroom floor. They fired her four weeks into the filming of *Tequila Road* and hired some French actress for the role. That sent her over the edge, I guess, and she drove her car straight into a canyon. It's amazing that she only suffered a concussion and some minor injuries."

"I read about that," Gingie said softly.

"She went into treatment again, and I was put in my father's custody. It was the first time I'd seen him in three years."

"Why didn't Vince take custody of you?" Gingie demanded.

"He would have, but since my own father was alive and well and willing to have me, that's where the courts sent me. Actually, it was my father's wife, Candy Jirrell, who wanted to take custody of me. They had a little girl — my sister, Lisa — and for a while Candy had these terribly domestic ideas about the four of us becoming a typical, all-American family." He rested his cheek against Gingie's hair and closed his eyes. Soft, she was so soft. And warm and comforting and sweet. None of the memories hurt as much with her head resting on his shoulder.

"But then my father went to Vegas, and Candy got a part in a weekly television drama, so the family thing kind of dried up. I wound up at home alone with Lisa, who was three at the time."

"So all of a sudden, you became her father and mother, as well as her brother," Gingie guessed.

"That's about it. I mean, she was such a cute little kid, you couldn't help but love her."

"Lisa must have thought the sun rose and set on you," Gingie murmured. How could Lisa have thought otherwise, with a handsome, lonely, loving big brother who gave her the time and attention that her parents wouldn't? "What happened when your mom got out of treatment?"

"There was a big scene. She wanted me to live with her again. God knows I didn't really like living with Candy and my father, but I didn't want to leave Lisa."

"What a terrible decision for a teenager to face," Gingie said sadly.

"Luckily, the decision was taken out of my hands. Vince, my father, and my mother's lawyer all convinced her that I would be the focus of even more scandal if she tried to get me back into custody. So in the end, I spent summers with her on Sontara and some weekends and holidays with her back in the States."

"When did you leave home? Did you go to college?" She felt him tense.

"Not exactly. I moved out when I was eighteen, but I didn't pursue my education. I had terrible grades in high school, and I was a restless, cocky, surly kid who figured no college could teach me anything I needed to know."

"What did you do then?" she persisted.

"I worked on and off for a film production company for a couple of years," he said vaguely.

"But you weren't happy?"

He shifted suddenly. "I think we began this conversation to talk about Vince, not me."

Gingie pulled away just enough to meet his gaze. "Is he in surgery right now?"

"Probably."

"How soon will we hear from Alice?"

"Not for at least a few hours."-

"Then we have plenty of time to kill, don't we?"

"Gingie . . ." He was suddenly acutely aware of the way she was draped across him, filling his arms with her warm, limber, long-legged vibrancy. As Roe and Gingie stared at each other, her eyes turned a slightly darker shade of blue, a smoky color that he was learning to recognize.

"Your scratches are almost healed," she murmured, lightly tracing her soft fingertips down his cheek, touching him as if there were no danger in it.

He grabbed her hand. "Don't touch me like that." He scowled a moment later, realizing with exasperation that he sounded like some virginal Gothic heroine.

She made it worse by immediately looking hurt. How could she change roles so easily, he wondered in desperation, going from smoky-eyed seductress to hurt puppy in the blink of an eye?

"I'm sorry," she mumbled. Looking as confused as she looked hurt, she pulled away from him a little more.

"Look, I don't mean to sound so . . ." His eyes dropped to the neckline of her shimmering, sea-colored dress. Her alabaster skin looked as smooth and flawless as fresh-cream, and the faint swell of her breasts made his mouth go dry.

"Gingie," he tried again, positive that a mature, experienced man should be able to handle this situation. "It's just not . . ."

Her lips were so full, and they looked so tender and warm. Her nose was too long for cover-girl beauty, and the sharpness of her cheekbones must have made her an angular-looking adolescent. She was heartbreak-ingly beautiful, and the way she shifted her legs and arched her back sent his senses into spontaneous combustion.

"It's not what?" she whispered, her expressive eyes now mostly hidden behind the thick veil of her dark lashes.

Her voice, hesitant and low, made him long to hear her whisper her secret desires to him beneath the rustling, sunbleached sheets on his bed. Unbidden images floated through his mind, sparking a darkly erotic flame of curiosity.

What would Gingie say to a man in private, having written some of the most intriguingly sensual lyrics of her generation? What would she ask for, having undoubtedly already received offers that Roe had never even thought of? What would her musical, honeyed voice sound like, helplessly lost in the depths of passion? What would her legs, which he had spent days trying in vain to ignore, feel like wrapped around him?

Would it be slow and tender between them, as her childlike vulnerability made him believe? Or would it be raw, sweaty, and wildly cathartic, as the sultry look in her eyes sometimes promised? Both possibilities excited him so much, he wasn't sure which he was hoping for.

And that was when he realized how dangerously close to the edge he had already traveled.

"Roe?" Gingie breathed. It didn't come out nearly as loud as she'd intended. She wasn't even sure he'd heard her. Her mouth was dry, and she almost felt like she was suffocating.

Roe's expression was dark and heavy-lidded, defying interpretation, but instinct told Gingie that every bit of his attention was focused on her. As still as a predator about to pounce, he seemed to be struggling internally. His breath gradually changed its rhythm, growing a little faster, and a dark flush stole across his cheeks. The moment their eyes met again, Gingie's breath increased to match speed with his, and something hot started flowing through her body, draining her of her usual exuberant strength and replacing it with a languor she had never experienced but could certainly identify.

"Oh, my God," she choked, the words barely making it past her lips. Suddenly her senses were flooded with him, with a thousand things she had, due to long habit, resisted dwelling upon until now.

His chest rose and fell in shallow breaths, its hard, smoothly curved pectoral muscles outlined against his shirt. His golden skin gleamed with a fine sheen of sweat, as if he had bicycled home very fast, and the effect was disturbingly erotic. His eyes were the color of the fine whiskey Milo enjoyed, and there was a feral gleam in them that made Gingie want to be devoured.

Blue-black hair fell over his forehead in thick, healthy waves, framing a face that could have made him as famous as either of his parents. She longed to touch his hair, ached to press her lips to the smooth hollow beneath his jaw.

His lips parted slightly, and Gingie felt the hunger he inexplicably stirred in her, the yearning he incited despite her deeply ingrained self-discipline. She looked quickly away from the irresistible temptation of his mouth and lowered her eyes again, wondering what to do about the whirlwind of feeling growing between them.

Looking at his body didn't ease the heavy pulsing in her abdomen. He was magnificently proportioned, and his faded clothes fit him like a second skin. His belly was flat, his hips narrow, his thighs smoothly muscled, and his . . . Gingie drew in a sharp breath as she realized the effect her fascinated stare had on him.

She made a little whimpering sound, more alarmed by her own physical turmoil than by the obvious evidence of his. *She didn't do this.*

"I don't . . ." She choked on the words. The instincts that she had always ruthlessly appropriated for her art were now ruling her. How could this be happening? What kind of wizardry did Roe possess?

"Shakespeare's sorcerer," she breathed suddenly, her thoughts disjointed and chaotic. "Prospero."

"Don't call me that." His voice was rough and sexy, almost a purr. He smoothed his palm across her bare thigh, slipping it boldly underneath the flimsy material of her little sundress.

Gingie gasped and started breathing as if she'd just run twenty miles. She *should* run twenty miles. Right now. Instead, she found herself leaning toward him, melting into the heat of his hard body, trembling almost violently as she teetered on the threshold between helpless yearning and superstitious fear.

"It's okay," he whispered, surprised by the fervor of her reaction. With slow strokes he explored the smooth, firm thigh beneath his palm. Despite the unmistakable passion glowing in her eyes, Roe also sensed her nervousness and uncertainty. Could she possibly doubt how desirable he found her? Following his instincts, he reassured her. "Your skin is like silk. Like . . . lotus oil, flower petals, fresh cream . . ." He squeezed gently, loving the warm, resilient feel of her flesh under his hands, aroused by the way her eyes closed as her lips parted and her head tilted back.

"Ohh," she sighed. "When you do that . . . it makes me dizzy."

"What, that?" He squeezed again. "Or that?" He shifted his hand to her inner thigh and let his finger slip teasingly along the elastic of her skimpy panties.

She collapsed forward, graceful even then, and wrapped her arms around his neck. Hungry for her, and a little dizzy himself, he sank down into the soft cushions of the couch and pulled her on top of him.

"That's good, too," she admitted, her voice higher and wispier than he'd ever heard it. .

He stretched his legs out and gripped her wide, seductive hips, adjusting the way she sprawled across him to get the maximum effect. He pressed their hips together, letting her feel the delicious discomfort she inspired in his body, and growled, "That's what you do to me. And it's not the first time."

"Really?" She met his eyes, too dangerously enthralled to feel embarrassed as he rubbed his palms over her bottom, caressing and kneading her firm cheeks, shifting provocatively beneath her.

"Oh, yeah," he muttered, his emery-board voice rasping delightfully along her senses.

She lowered her mouth to his, overwhelmed by the waves of delight that he sent washing over her. Warm and soft, his lips parted instantly for her, and his tongue coaxed her mouth open with a lazy, enticing stroke. His kiss was hot and deep, long and demanding and ruthlessly skillful. It wasn't fair, she thought vaguely. The way his lips rubbed moistly against her cheek, her eyelids, and her throat without pausing long enough for her to draw a deep breath, made coherent thoughts impossible. The way his tongue thrust silkily into her mouth to duel with her own, teasing and tickling, proved that he knew too much about women to even consider playing fair.

Her whole body melted bonelessly under his restless, knowing touch, and she moved her hips, rubbing boldly against him as she was guided by the strong hands on her bottom. He responded without inhibition, adjusting her position to slide their bodies even closer together, whispering hotly to her when the denim-covered bulge pressing snugly against her pelvis stirred and grew harder.

Their mouths melded again, wetly, greedily, more insistently than before. Gingie clutched his shoulder, reveling in the bunch and flow of muscle beneath her fingers as he wrapped his arms around her to stroke her hair, her shoulders, the nape of her neck, the small of her back.

A long sigh escaped her, ending on a startled groan as he pushed up the hem of her dress, slid his palm into the valley between her legs, and cupped the soft, feminine mound there, delicately stroking her with his long, deft fingers. A sharp sensation of pleasure splintered through Gingie so suddenly that her thighs clamped together involuntarily, imprisoning him, and he paused in his fevered kisses long enough to give her a slow, wicked grin. His coaxing murmurs and the expression on his face turned her insides to molasses even more surely than the delicious, rhythmic play of his fingers against the thin, overheated fabric of her panties.

Ready to throw years of carefully considered behavior to the winds without hesitation, Gingie panted, "Maybe I can, after all."

"Oh, honey," Roe said on a heartfelt groan. He squeezed gently, understanding the need to be tender with the most sensitive part of her body. She was hot, and he could feel her dampness even through her cotton panties. "You definitely can."

Gingie sighed and kissed him again. Her blond hair was soft against his cheek, her thighs made a warm cocoon around his hand as he sought ways to excite her, and her mouth was as sweet as almond wine. Even in his fantasies, he hadn't known it would be like this between them.

She started fumbling at the buttons of his shirt. When she dropped one leg to the floor for balance, he played more insistently on her senses, loving the throaty sounds she made and the restless way she shifted. When her squirming became too delightful, he gritted his teeth for a desperate moment, then shifted her slightly and used both hands to start unfastening her dress.

"What's wrong?" she murmured when he grumbled against her throat in exasperation.

"The tassels have gotten all tangled up in the hooks. Don't you ever wear simple clothes?"

She laughed and arched her back, rubbing her small breasts against him. His hands shook, and he abandoned the task of undressing her to cover her breasts with his palms, rubbing them across her sensitive nipples.

"Oh, that almost hurts," Gingie sighed. Her head lolled forward and she stroked his hands with trembling fingers.

"Oh, Gingie." He wrapped an arm around her waist to draw her up higher and kissed a pebble-hard nipple through the fabric of her dress. Still unsatisfied, he gently nipped it, then lifted her breast with his palm and circled it with kisses, desperate to taste and touch her naked body. "I've wanted to do this since the hotel in Trápani."

"Really?" Her voice was slurred.

"You must have known." He turned his attention to her other breast.

"I . . . *Ohh.* "

"Help me get this off you," he insisted, tugging at her tangled fringe and Victorian hooks.

"Ahh . . . Just do that once more."

He smiled against the soft skin revealed by her neckline. "Only if you'll take this damn thing off, then."

"Okay. *Oh, yes.* Like that." A breathless moment later, she murmured against his ear, "Or you could just tear it off me."

Her husky voice and the whisper of his own fantasies clouded his mind. His hands were braced at the neckline of her pretty dress, ready to rip it off her delectable body, when the shrill ring of the phone made them both jump like they'd been stung.

They stared stupidly at each other, as if suddenly waking up in the middle of a deep, dream-filled sleep.

The second ring brought a wave of stunned surprise with it. The third brought shock, and the fourth brought a flood of confusion and uncertainty. Gingie tried to slide away from Roe on the fifth ring, and he gripped her arms tightly on the sixth, holding her in place. Halfway through the seventh ring, someone else apparently answered the phone. Gingie and Roe kept staring at each other, their harsh breaths slicing across the silence.

Gingie spoke at last. Her voice was low and strained. "I . . . I can't do this with you."

His eyes narrowed. He tried to bring his spinning senses to a standstill. "You were making a pretty good stab at it."

"I'm sorry," she said helplessly. "I don't do this."

"I don't get it." He drew a deep breath. It didn't help much, so he drew another one.

She could see what this sudden imposition of self-control was costing him. He looked as though he'd been hit in the belly with a two-by-four. It made her feel terribly guilty. "It's my fault."

He blinked. "What's your fault? This?" He was starting to sound irritable.

"I should have . . . I shouldn't have . . ."

With his hands still holding her firmly, he let his head drop back onto the sofa and closed his eyes. "Damn it."

Still sprawled atop him, her clothing in disarray, Gingie said, "You don't understand."

"I sure as hell don't."

"It's complicated, but I can explain."

"I don't think I can handle one of your explanations at the moment, Gingie," he said sincerely.

"Ordinarily, this doesn't happen to me."

"No, of course not," he responded, aware of the martyred tone in his voice.

"I got carried away."

"I know. That was the good part." He released her at last and draped an arm across his face. His voice was muffled as he said, "Maybe you should leave me alone now, Gingie."

"But I just feel so bad about this!" she brushed some dark hair off his forehead.

"Don't touch me like that." He snorted a moment later. "Didn't I already say that? You should have listened to me."

"Please look at me, Roe," she pleaded.

"Believe me, it's better if I don't right now."

"Do you know how I've accumulated all those top-ten albums and singles?" she began in disjointed desperation.

"I don't want to talk about your career right now," he said emphatically. "Please get off me."

"I'm trying to explain something important to you!" Intent on getting his full attention, she pulled his arm away from his face.

"Damn it, isn't it bad enough yet?" he growled. "Do you want to tear me apart?"

A moment later his arms were around her again, drawing her against him with ruthless strength, and the raw demand of his kiss drove the air from her lungs. Before she knew how it had happened, she'd forgotten what she'd meant to explain, and her hands were in his hair, her breasts were rubbing against his chest, and her thigh was pressing against the juncture of his legs, teasing him in a way she instinctively knew would make him delirious.

Neither of them heard the door opening, but the sound of Milo's voice reached them loud and clear a moment later. "Gingie? Are you in — Holy smoke!"

They broke apart like guilty teenagers. Hauling breath into his burning lungs, Roe rolled his head to look at the man in the doorway. The man who lived with Gingie.

"Well, knock me over with a feather!" Milo exclaimed. His expression was unreadable behind his rose-colored glasses.

"Um . . ." Gingie said.

Roe wisely chose to say nothing.

"I'm shocked!" Milo nodded, as if verifying this statement for them. "Yes, I have to say, I'm definitely shocked. Stunned! *Amazed.* Who'd have thought it?" He shook his head and leaned against the doorframe to study them at his leisure.

Gingie made a choking sound. Coming down to earth, Roe took his hand off her bottom. Then he wasn't sure what to do with it.

Milo folded his arms. The faint quirk of his lips gave Roe the strangest feeling that the musician was actually *enjoying* himself. Refusing to look at either man, Gingie glanced distractedly around her, as if suddenly surprised to find herself in this room, not to mention in Roe's arms, with her leg resting intimately between his and her skin flushed and glowing. His heart twisted when he saw how lovely passion made her look.

"Look, kids," Milo said jovially, "I am mortified to have interrupted, but didn't you guys even notice the phone ringing?"

"The phone?" Gingie said like a slow child. Then, more securely, "The phone."

"Who was it?" Roe asked, trying to remember the last time he'd been in such an awkward position.

"Whoofie and the Doctor."

"Is it about Vince's surgery?" Gingie asked quickly.

Milo lowered his glasses to peer at Gingie for a moment. "You know about that?"

Suddenly gathering strength, Gingie sprang to her feet. "Roe just told me!"

"Ah, is that what he was doing?" Milo slid his glasses back into place. "I wasn't sure."

"You knew about Vince, and you didn't tell me?" Gingie stalked forward, her voice vibrating with outraged accusation. "How could you keep a thing like that from me?"

"He didn't want me to tell you. *I* only found out because I'm so nosy," Milo protested.

"And were you *ever* going to tell me?"

Roe sat up and straightened his shirt. He considered standing for a moment but decided his sitting position provided better camouflage for his embarrassingly persistent physical condition.

"I was going to tell you after the surgery," Milo explained. "After the worst was over."

"That's not your right!" Gingie shouted at Milo. "I'm an adult. How dare you hide things from me, as if I wasn't capable of handling bad news! I'm sick of people coddling me and baby-sitting me!"

"I'm . . ." Milo looked at Roe for a moment, as if seeking support there. At last he said, "Well, hell, I'm sorry, Gin. We've all just always . . . you know."

After a heavy silence, Gingie sank into the hard wooden chair by the desk and said, "Yes, I know." She sighed and added, "I'm sorry I shouted at you, Milo. It's just that . . . things need to be different now."

With a telling, rose-colored glance in Roe's direction, Milo said, "Evidently."

"Who are Whoofie and the Doctor?" Roe asked at last.

"My back-up vocalist and my percussionist," Gingie said.

"Why did they call?" Roe persisted.

"They're here on Sontara," Milo said. "They missed the ferry but convinced some sucker to bring them over in his fishing boat."

"Probably my cousin," Roe said morosely. "I guess they want to stay here?"

"Well, there's still an empty bedroom for Whoofie," Milo said, "and I think the couch in the *salone* is good enough for the Doctor. If you don't mind, that is, Roe."

"Oh, what the hell, call me Prospero." Sometimes the only thing to do was to surrender gracefully.

Seven

"Have you seen the tabloids?" Vince demanded. His voice, slurred by drugs and fueled by outrage, crackled hollowly across the unstable connection from New York to Sontara.

Having learned two nights ago that Vince's surgery had gone exactly as planned, Roe was now rather sorry that the phones were still working. "No, of course not, Vince. We don't get stuff like that here. You know that."

"Then let me read you a few sample headlines from today's selection." Despite his weak condition and steady supply of painkillers, Vince managed to make his voice cut like a knife. Roe had an uneasy suspicion that he knew what was coming next. "'Gingie Shacks Up with Italian Film Star's Renegade Son,'" Vince began. He continued, "'Notorious Rock Star Hiding Out with Sicilian Mystery Man.' Both of these headlines," Vince added, his voice getting louder. "are accompanied by rather flattering shots of Gingie smiling beatifically at you and surrounded, for some inexplicable reason, by armed guards and military men."

The airport. Roe sighed. "Vince, I can ex —"

"No, no, let me read you my favorite," his brother interrupted with horrible sarcasm. "'Gingie Meets Elvis in Secret Mediterranean Love Nest.'"

"Elvis?" Roe repeated incredulously.

"Needless to say, the photograph appears to have been doctored. Would you like to hear the article about Gingie's near arrest on smuggling charges?"

"Vince, you don't un —"

"How could you have let this happen?" Vince raged. "You were supposed to keep her out of trouble!"

"There was a photographer at the airport," Roe shot back. "Maybe he knew about Gingie because you let her get on the plane in New York wearing that skintight outfit with all the zippers!"

"That's the most inconspicuous thing she owns!" Vince bellowed.

"Haven't you noticed?"

"Well, yes," Roe admitted more calmly. "I have."

"I'm supposed to be recuperating from major surgery!" Vince cried. "How can you let her traumatize me like this?"

"How can *you* send Sandy Stephen, Milo Wake, Whoofie, and the Doctor here without even warning me?" Roe demanded angrily.

"I couldn't get a call through to Sontara. Sandy was hysterical, and Milo decided to take him to Sontara just to annoy me!" Vince's voice was rising in pitch. "Then Whoofie and the Doctor became incensed when they found out that Milo and Gingie were enjoying a seaside holiday when they were all supposed to be doing a television appearance in Chicago, and they —"

"All right, calm down, you're getting hysterical yourself," Roe warned.

"I *can't* calm down! How can I spend a month recuperating when you've let Gingie run wild in just one week?"

"Run wild?" Roe said impatiently. He was beginning to sympathize with Gingie. His brother seemed to have become even more tyrannical over the years, in his own wellmeaning way. "All right, so the most notorious woman in pop music got photographed with the son of a couple of other celebrities, and the scandalmongers are milking it because it's been a slow week. Get a little perspective, Vince. It's no big deal."

"Oh, Roe, you're so naïve. You don't really think this will be the end of it, do you?" Vince groaned.

"At the moment, Vince, I'm more concerned with the way my house is filling up with refugees from the video channel. The whole village is in an uproar."

"I believe you." Vince sighed. "I'm sorry, Roe. Maybe it was a dreadful mistake to send Gingie there. She creates an uproar wherever she goes. I should have known better than to hope she would stay out of trouble on Sontara."

"You're getting uptight about nothing, Vince. Gingie hasn't caused any trouble, and I guess the villagers will quiet down in another week or so." Roe rolled his eyes and wondered why the hell he was defending her. After two totally sleepless nights and two days of unbearable tension, he should have finally exhausted the last of his patience. And Gingie *was* causing trouble. He just didn't like the way Vince overreacted, making himself ill and making Gingie sound like some kind of drunken, insensitive, freewheeling party girl. "Just take it easy, Vince. Do you get like this every time Gingie's name appears in print?"

"Not when she's written up for winning awards, breaking sales records, or contributing to charity. I only get upset," Vince explained woefully, "when she alienates record companies, smuggles homeopathic remedies across international borders, and gets photographed in compromising positions with men who should know better."

"Do you know what this reminds me of?" Roe challenged, getting annoyed again. "This reminds me of all those fights we had when Mom was alive."

"All right, all right, point taken." Vince sighed. "But Gingie isn't like Mom. Gingie isn't like anyone else on planet Earth."

"I've noticed that," Roe said dryly. "But the best thing for you to do is forget all about her for the next few weeks. Don't read, watch, or listen to anything that might upset you, and don't worry about Gingie. I'll take good care of her."

Roe stared dumbly at the receiver after he hung up. He realized with belated self-disgust that he had just thrown away a sterling opportunity to get Gingie and her entourage out of his life. With just a sentence or two, he could have convinced Vince to give him carte blanche to throw his growing collection of rock musicians out of his house and off Sontara.

Instead, he had just promised to take care of Gingie until Vince was completely recovered. What the hell was the matter with him? It wasn't as if he *wanted* her here. After their scene in the study, he wanted to get as far away from her as humanly possible.

Gingie's voice crooned melodically as Roe made his way through the house and out into the midday sun. It wasn't her, actually, it was a recording. Gingie herself eschewed the narcissism so consistently displayed by Roe's father, and she played other performers' music rather than her own. Whoofie, however, had put a stop to that, having arrived with tapes of every recording Gingie and her band had ever made.

Whoofie was a beautiful black woman in her late twenties, with a petite, curvaceous figure and an impressive headful of long cornrows; Roe couldn't decide whether or not they were real. The Doctor waved jovially to Roe as he joined them on the terrace, apparently having forgiven Roe for referring to him as a "drummer" yesterday. The Doctor, whose PhD was in anthropological musicology, wanted it clearly understood from the outset that he was a *percussionist.*

Milo had engaged both musicians in a game of Montana Red and was winning. Roe suspected he was cheating, but said nothing. Gingie was in the village. Roe had told her that the customs officials at Punta Ráisi had phoned the day before to say her collection of homeopathic remedies should be arriving on the morning ferry to Sontara. She had decided to walk to town, and Sandy had silently gone with her.

It was the only time Roe had spoken to her alone since Milo had discovered them together in the study. He didn't want to get involved with a rock star, and he didn't like the way she kept changing her mind about what she wanted from him. He had successfully avoided speaking to her alone for the past couple of days — Sandy made that relatively easy by being her constant shadow. The more people appeared at the villa, the more nervous the kid became, and the more he clung to Gingie.

Maria Sellerio was equally nervous lately, tripping over her own feet and not answering Roe's questions unless he repeated himself three or four times. Her gaze, Roe had noticed, settled most often on Sandy. Poor Maria. She was pretty and sweet, but she was no match for Gingie.

Gingie's voice vibrated sensually all around Roe, since the Doctor had helped Whoofie position the speakers for maximum effect. *At the First Sign of Trouble,* Whoofie explained to Roe as he gazed down at the beach, had been Gingie's fifth big hit.

"This is the chorus, Roe," Whoofie called eagerly over her shoulder before returning her attention to the card game.

"Come on, ante up," Milo urged her impatiently.

"You can hear me really well here, Roe," she added.

"That's nice," Roe said mildly. Narcissistic, yes, but basically nice, he thought. He braced himself against the caressing, longing sound of Gingie's voice as it swelled into the chorus. She was incredibly gifted, he acknowledged.

Avoiding Gingie was easy, but ignoring her was not. He kept away from the house as much as possible, but he couldn't stop thinking about her. Her kisses, her sighs, and the hungry, affectionate touch of her hands had all stirred something in him that would not be put back to sleep. His heart went out to her when he realized how hurt she was by Vince's lack of trust in her, and he couldn't help but admire the way she made everyone around her feel happy and important.

Shy Maria obviously idolized her, and Roe was convinced his young cousin Gaspare was in love with Gingie. Sandy clearly couldn't get comfortable with anyone but Gingie, timidly avoiding conversation or eye contact with anyone else, and even Milo, relentlessly cynical and sarcastic, softened around Gingie.

Roe had felt Milo's speculative, amused gaze on him several times during the past couple of days, and it made him extremely uncomfortable. Consequently, Milo was someone else he avoided.

The villagers, as Roe had indicated to Vince, were indeed in an uproar, suspicious about what kind of wild orgy Gingie and her long-haired friends were enjoying in Adelina Marino's villa. Roe had spent most of yesterday morning denying rumors, having gone to the village only to enjoy a cappuccino in peace and quiet. His restful hideaway had become busier than Grand Central Station. If Vince was right, Roe thought wryly, Gingie would have the same effect on the remotest parts of the Okavango Delta.

When Gingie's voice finally faded and died away, Roe breathed deeply and closed his eyes, lost somewhere between masochistic enjoyment of this torture and exhausted relief. The ubiquitous sound of her voice was like a love potion, making him yearn for her until his skin felt hot and his mind grew cloudy.

"Whoofie, are you playing this game, or what?" Milo prodded.

"I just want to turn over the tape."

Coming to his senses, Roe turned around and said, "Let's give it a rest, Whoofie."

"Yeah, give it a rest for Roe's sake," Milo chimed in. Some smirking quality in his voice made Roe look sharply at him, but his expression was obscured by his glasses.

A moment later, they heard Gingie's voice again. Feeling haunted, Roe crossed the terrace and walked under the vine-covered arch that led to the dusty road. He found her there, sitting in Zu Aspanu's donkey cart. She and the old man were singing together. The song was one of those old Sicilian ballads whose minor key wailing gave ample evidence of the centuries of foreign domination in Sicily. The lyrics of the song, which were in dialect, sounded vaguely Arabic, like the tune.

Zu Aspanu croaked off-key, while Gingie's beautiful voice carried a sensual exoticism that made the song, which Roe had always hated, sound strangely charming. She laughed delightedly when they had finished the last note, then clapped for Zu Aspanu, complimenting him on his fine performance.

"She learns faster than a speeding bullet!" Zu Aspanu told Roe delightedly as he helped Gingie off the cart. "I sing it for her once and she learns everything — the music, the Sicilian words, everything!"

"Pretty impressive," Roe admitted. "By the end of the month, you'll speak better Italian than I do."

"Oh, I can only sing in other languages," Gingie explained. "I can't speak them. It's a different talent."

"Well, I speak five languages but can't sing in a single one of them, so I guess we're evenly matched." He began unloading parcels from the heavily laden donkey cart. "What did you buy? I thought you were only going to collect your medicine box in town."

"Thank you for convincing them to give this back to me, Roe," she said as he handed the remedy box to her. "It seems like you can do anything."

Her sparkling smile and sun-kissed cheeks made him stare, his heart thudding heavily in his chest. The sudden wave of heat that assaulted him would go away, he was sure, if only he could hug her to him, feel that limber, long-legged body press affectionately against him, and maybe give her a quick kiss.

Her gaze held captive by the sudden, golden glitter in his eyes, Gingie swayed unthinkingly toward Roe. If only he would touch her, maybe just give her a brief hard hug, surely she would lose this extremely inconvenient, distracting, and painful ache she felt almost all the time these days. Their bodies brushed for a brief, tantalizing dangerous moment before Zu Aspanu called cheerfully from the other side of the cart, "What did she buy, you ask? Hah! She paid through the nose for all these groceries, but she bought goodwill for a song!"

Roe blinked. Gingie lowered her head and stepped back. "I, uh, I was thinking about what you said to me the other day." Heat flooded her face as every detail of what happened in the study flashed through her mind with burning intensity. *Oh, Roe, what should I do about you?*

"What I said?" His voice was husky, clinging to her senses.

"I thought that the best way to save you any more trouble," she began, "would be to put a stop to any rumors myself. So when I saw Zu Aspanu awaiting the morning ferry, I asked him to take me around to meet all the shopkeepers and —"

"And she was so charming!" Zu Aspanu explained, pulling boxes of fresh fruit and vegetables out of the cart. "Now they are all sweetness and light."

"Yes, everyone assures me that they never really thought anything immoral was going on out here, and they're sure my friends are just as nice as I am." She gestured toward the bags and boxes of groceries and household goods. "Anyhow, I couldn't just walk out of all those shops without buying anything so . . ."

"Oh, Gingie." Roe grinned, taking her breath away. "You *are* a strategist. God alone knows why Vince doesn't believe you can look after yourself." Roe wondered when *he* had started believing it.

"You're pleased, then?" she asked hesitantly.

"Of course." Unable to resist, he touched her cheek with one forefinger, then ran his knuckles along her chin. "I should have thought of it myself. How could they resist you?"

She closed her eyes, losing herself in the bliss of his touch. For two whole days he'd barely looked at her, much less laid a finger on her. It was driving her crazy.

"It all comes out in the wash," Zu Aspanu said complacently.

"Then we sat at the café in the Piazza. Don Ciccio's oldest grandson was there with his guitar, and I sang a few of my songs for everyone. Then your uncle offered to teach me some Silician songs . . ." She shrugged and smiled again, sorry Roe had taken his hand away. "And here we are."

They stared at each other again, before Roe finally said, "Where's Sandy?" He had just realized the boy wasn't with them.

Gingie frowned in puzzlement. "He said he had to meet someone and disappeared. Isn't that strange?"

Seeing her concern, Roe said, "Don't worry. The island's too small for him to get lost."

As they scooped up the groceries and headed into the house, Gingie said, "There's just one problem with all this food I bought."

"What's that, Gingie?"

"It's all raw, and I don't really know how to cook."

"Somehow, I expected that." He remembered what Milo had said. "I guess Maria can do something with all of this. Is she still here?"

"No, she left a couple of hours ago. Don't worry, Gingie, I'm sure Milo can think of something to do with it."

*I*t would take them, Milo asserted, a week to eat everything Gingie had bought, and that was only if Gaspare and Zu Aspanu helped them. Roe's uncle, however, couldn't be convinced to eat anything but his precious peanut butter, and so he went home shortly before lunch.

It was during the siesta hour of sleep and shadowplay, when the whole villa was mercifully silent and the lemon groves released their scent to the harsh Sicilian sun, that Gingie sought out Roe.

"I've been looking for you," she murmured, finding him relaxing in a hammock which rested in the shadows beneath a fig tree at the edge of the terrace.

His eyes narrowed as he studied her. He had told her to cover her shoulders and knees before going to the village, and she had complied. The results, however, were not what he'd had in mind. Her red skirt with its black polka dots ended mid-thigh. The voluminous black lace which was attached to it, and which comprised the rest of her skirt, hung well past her knees with enticing transparence, giving him shadowy glimpses of her long legs every time she moved. Her matching red blouse was appropriately high-necked and long-sleeved, but it ended just below her cupcake breasts, leaving her taut stomach bare.

He considered explaining to her why this outfit was no more conservative than any of her others, but finally decided it wasn't worth the effort. By all accounts, the villagers loved her now, which wasn't too surprising. Anyhow, she looked wonderful in that absurd getup. Her sit-ups, he noted through the veil of his dark lashes, had really paid off.

"You look very pensive," she murmured.

"I was just thinking about a cigarette," he lied. His voice sounded a little gravelly.

"A cigarette? Does Milo's smoking bother you? I'm always arguing with him about it."

He shrugged. "You're right, it's a nasty habit. But it doesn't really bother me. I used to be a pretty heavy smoker."

"Really? And you quit?"

He nodded. "While I was lying in a body cast in the hospital in Gaborone, after being trampled by a hippo." He smiled and closed his eyes, enjoying the gentle sway of the hammock and the way his blood thrummed with life when Gingie knelt near him. "By the time I got to Cairo and was able to move my arms again, I decided it was best not to start again. I could never smoke, or do anything else, in moderation. Hereditary trait, I guess."

"Vince is a heavy smoker," Gingie said. "So is your father. I'm surprised he can still sing, actually."

"You've met him?" He opened his eyes again.

"Once. We gave out a few awards together at some ceremony. He smoked four cigarettes backstage in about fifteen minutes."

"How'd you get along?" he asked curiously.

"Oh . . ." She hesitated, not sure how to answer. However, since she was always truthful, she finally admitted, "I guess he was a little hard to take, Roe, if you'll forgive me for saying so."

"Oh, I forgive you. Was he rude to you?" The thought angered him more than he would have thought possible after all these years. If Jordan had hurt Gingie's feelings . . .

"No, not really. It was a pleasure to meet him and everything, since he's been around for years —"

"If you said that to him, no wonder you two didn't get along. One of the reasons he never wants to see me is that he hates being reminded that he's old enough to have a thirty-four-year-old son."

"Really?" Gingie was shocked. "But I would think he'd be proud of you! You're so accomplished and interesting, smart and experienced. You're kind and patient, not to mention brave."

Embarrassed, Roe quickly asked, "If you didn't remind him of his age, then what happened?"

Gingie hesitated again. "Well, I don't mean to sound vain or anything, Roe, but I was the number-one vocalist in the country that year, my third album had just gone platinum, and I'd won my fourth Grammy just a few weeks before your father and I met. But he treated me like I was some wide-eyed insignificant groupie who should be utterly thrilled to meet him and flattered to be allowed to hand out a few awards with him." Remembering Jordan Hunter's condescension, she said, "I don't mean to be offensive, Roe, but I thought his attitude was a little out of place for a fading singer who hasn't had a gig outside of Las Vegas in ten years."

"You can be a little ruthless, after all," Roe said in surprise.

"Oh, I didn't say anything like that to his face, despite the way he acted," she protested. "And maybe I shouldn't have said it to you. I mean, now I've criticized your brother and your father. You must think I'm a witch."

He chuckled and touched her hair. "Oh, Gingie. No one could think that of you. Not even Signora Gambarossa." Aware of the shiver of excitement that shook him when he touched her, he drew his hand away quickly. "My father is just a devout narcissist, Gingie. And he's very threatened by any woman who's more gifted than he is. I don't suppose I realized that that was a major stumbling block in his relationship with my mother until after she died. He had a few hot years of success when they were first married, but he was never the brilliant talent that she was, and I think that was always pretty clear. In fact, she was probably the only person who ever tried to pretend otherwise, for his sake."

"That's such a shame," Gingie said with feeling. "That he wanted her to be less than she was, I mean." Roe's arm dangled next to her, tempting her, as he rocked gently in the hammock. Unable to resist, she traced his knuckles with her fingertips. It was so good to touch him again. "I need your help," she said desperately.

Aroused by the silken touch of her fingertips and startled by the sudden seriousness in her tone, he rolled on his side to look at her. "Is something wrong?" he asked softly. Why did he feel as if he'd do anything for her? Her eyes were misty, and it twisted his heart.

"Sort of," she acknowledged. "I have to talk to someone, and you're the only person I can think of."

"Is it about Vince?" he probed. When she shook her head, he leaned forward and asked, "Then what's bothering you?"

She took the plunge. "I'm trying to decide if I should go to bed with you."

Roe fell out of the hammock. For a moment, as he flailed for balance, he thought he might save himself from humiliation, but an instant later his most vulnerable body part hit the ground with a resounding thud as he crashed to earth.

"Oh, Roe!" Gingie cried, crawling beside him and searching him for broken bones. "Are you all right? Oh, no!"

"Don't touch me there," he said through gritted teeth.

"But I just want to make sure —"

"It's still in working order, don't worry," he snapped.

"But you landed right on that rock —"

"Damn it, damn it, damn it!" Nauseated by the pain, he scraped himself off the ground and sat leaning against the tree.

"You're kind of green," Gingie said in concern.

"It'll pass." He took a steadying breath. "Gingie, Gingie, you shouldn't shock me like that. I'm not as young as I used to be."

"I'm sorry," she apologized woefully. "I just thought I should be truthful."

"That's . . . very commendable," he said in a strangled voice.

"Can I get you anything? Some ice, maybe?"

"Good God, no." He closed his eyes. "Just try to hold still for a few minutes without doing anything unpredictable."

"I . . . Okay." It seemed a small enough request.

After a few agonized moments, Roe finally said, "Now, let me get this straight. You want me to help you decide if we should sleep together?"

"It's just that I need to talk about this, and it's really no one else's business."

He stared at her, wondering with bewilderment why that should make so much sense to him. "I see."

"And it's a pretty big decision for me," she added.

"Really?" It was hard to believe, considering her reputation.

"You see . . ." She licked her lips, so lush and pink. "I've always been very rigorous about my celibacy."

He was glad he was sitting on the ground for that one. "What?"

"I mean, it's really become part of my regime," she continued, looking rather embarrassed. "I exercise two hours every day, I eat right, I don't drink or smoke, I don't put stimulants or depressants into my body, I have a massage and a sauna once a week, and I . . ." She gestured vaguely toward him.

"You don't have sex?" he said incredulously. It was the one thing Roe had *never* contemplated giving up.

"That's right," she said, relieved he'd gotten the picture so quickly. "So —"

"Wait a minute," he said irritably. "You're putting me on."

"No, of course not." So much for getting the picture.

"Gingie, you've got two men staying here who came five thousand miles to be with you. I know Milo lives with you, he told me so himself."

"Well, everyone knows that." She scowled at him. "But I would have thought that you, of all people, would know better than to listen to gossip or jump to conclusions."

"I don't . . ." He sighed. "Never mind."

"Even if I didn't have a . . . a very specific way of life, I'd never sleep with Milo. I love him dearly, Roe, but he's shockingly cavalier in his treatment of women."

"Really?" Roe asked weakly.

"Just look at the way he dumped my sister twelve years ago because of a few minor political disagreements. After all, she wasn't asking him to *help* her seize the administrative buildings at Ann Arbor."

"Gingie . . ."

"And he's already been through three divorces, not to mention several messy —"

"It sounds like he could be in *my* family." Roe shook his head and asked, "So why does he live with you?"

"He had nowhere else to go. He's broke."

"How can he be broke?" Roe demanded. "He works for one of the most successful singers in the business."

"He's paying alimony to two of his ex-wives, and his last divorce was extremely nasty. Then a woman in Dallas decided to sue him for breach of promise. Well, Milo insists he never would have promised *anything* to someone who lives in Dallas, but th —"

"Never mind," Roe said wearily. "I get the picture. So you took him in?"

"That's right. Camilla was living with me at the time, teaching at Columbia. She and Milo didn't get along, though, so she moved out. Now Letitia lives with us."

"The homeopath."

"That's right. Oh, that's another thing I don't do."

"What?" he said in confusion.

"I don't let doctors give me painkillers and antibiotics and things like that. Letitia says —"

"Not just now, Gingie." He shifted his body slightly and found, to his relief, that it didn't hurt anymore. "And Sandy?"

"Sandy? Well, a couple of years ago, Sandy was just some shy kid working in his father's grocery store in Oregon and singing at a local club where all his school friends hung out. A manager saw him, signed him, and promoted him. Within six months, Sandy had become the number-one act in the country, with thousands of women screaming for his body and throwing themselves at him everywhere he went." She confided, "I think it's unbalanced him."

"How did you meet him?"

"His manager asked me to go to a *Rolling Stone* party with him, since Sandy wouldn't go alone." She shrugged. "He feels safe around me. I know some people think he's a little dull, but I really like him, Roe. And he's having such a hard time. People are so envious of success, but it can be an enormous burden."

"I . . . remember."

"That's right," she said softly. "Your mother never got used to it, did she?" When Roe shook his head, she continued, "By the time Sandy was nineteen, he couldn't walk down any street in America without hundreds of women trying to tear his clothes off. Two dozen photographers virtually live right outside his front door. He's having a little trouble adjusting."

"But he does all that kinky stuff on stage," Roe prodded.

Gingie shrugged. "His stage persona is just . . . a stage persona."

"What about you?" Roe asked for a moment. "Doesn't it all get to you?"

Gingie thought about it. "No, not really. I spent eight years working my way to the top. I knew exactly what I was getting into, and it was all I ever wanted. I don't care what they say about me. The music is all that counts."

"Those eight years must have been awfully rough," he probed.

"They were, but I knew I was only good at one thing in the whole world, so it wasn't like I had a lot of options. Anyhow, my parents always made it very clear that I could come home and start over whenever I wanted to." She smiled. "They thought maybe I'd settle for getting a degree in musicology. Like the Doctor."

"But you couldn't settle?"

"No," she said emphatically. "I wanted the whole world to hear my songs. And the burdens that go with being famous . . ." She shrugged and admitted, "It can be lonely, but I have my family, my friends, the band. And it was lonely even in the old days, night after night on the road. I toured nonstop from the time I was nineteen until I was twenty-seven."

"Being on the road all of the time doesn't leave any room for relationships," Roe said, thinking about his own life, too.

"No. And I didn't want desperate one-night stands or frantic tumbles in anonymous hotel rooms. Anyhow, all I really cared about or thought about was my work. All my energy went into my music, and my only real desire was to be the best."

"But you're on top of the world now, and you're not always on tour anymore," he said.

"No, but my life is still a grind, Roe. I write an album, record it, make the videos, tour to promote it, then start writing another." She shrugged. "And who can I trust, anyhow? Now that I'm famous, most men just see me as some blond rock idol who conjures up their sexual fantasies under the spotlight." She shook her head. "It's too confusing for me. Some men want to sleep with a rock star. Others want to know what it's like to be alone with *Gingie.* And then there are men like your father, who want me to pretend to be less than I am in order to pacify their egos. Men who also resent me for making ten times as much money as they do."

Roe thought it over. Then, distracted by her fragrance and the exquisite swell of her breasts beneath her tight blouse, he asked huskily, "So how long have you been practicing celibacy?"

"Thirty-one years."

"What?" Roe choked on his surprise. "You . . . You've never . . . You mean to tell me that you're a . . ." He forged ahead and said incredulously, "You're a *virgin?*" When she nodded, he protested, "But, Gingie, that's impossible!"

Of all the reactions she had expected from him, this wasn't among them. "Of course it isn't."

"But you're . . . You . . . It's not . . ." He leaned his head against the tree and tried to formulate a coherent thought. "You are, without a doubt, the sexiest woman I've ever known. How can that be, if you've never . . . if you're completely . . ."

"I've channeled all my sexual energy into my work," she explained reasonably.

"You're kidding me." He met her gaze again. "You're not kidding me," he said morosely. "You really mean it."

"Of course I mean it. This is not intended to amuse you, Roe."

"Believe me, it doesn't," he said with sincerity.

"And the problem is —"

"I know what the problem is," he interrupted.

"You do?" she said hopefully.

"Our bodies have been talking to each other since you got here, and you don't know what to do about it. I thought . . . Never mind what I thought, it doesn't matter now."

"But what shall we do? You're more experienced than I am," she added innocently.

Roe wanted a cigarette, a shot of whiskey, and a few other things he'd given up over the years. How had he stumbled into this mess?

"What I *want* to do is take you to bed and make love till we both pass out." Seeing her face flush and her jaw drop, c he added, "What I *should* do is get you the hell out of my house. However, I promised Vince I'd look after you. So what you and I are *going* to do, Gingie, is avoid each other like the plague. Have you got that?"

"But, Roe —"

"Because the last thing I need," he said, hauling himself to his feet, "is to keep losing sleep over a trouble-prone rock star who's some kind of . . . radical celibate. I have enough problems at the moment. Understood?"

"But I —"

"Good." He left her sitting there and descended angrily to the beach. His body aching in a different and increasingly familiar way, he stripped down to his shorts and dived into the ocean, hoping some hard exertion in the icy water would solve at least one of his problems, if only temporarily.

Eight

"*T*his is getting to be too much like *The Tempest*," Roe grumbled. He lay in the midday sun, wondering how things had gotten so wildly out of control.

His usually isolated, empty beach was covered with bodies — Milo, Sandy, Whoofie, the Doctor, Gaspare, and a few teenagers who had convinced Gaspare to bring them along. Out in the ocean, there lurked an unidentified boat. Roe was experienced enough to know that the people on board, whether reporters or simply rock fans, had their binoculars trained on this beach.

Gingie was the only person missing from the scene. She had gone into town with Zu Aspanu, having received an interview request from an American journalist who had recently married a Sicilian and now lived in Palermo. Since the woman's professional reputation was excellent, Roe had agreed with Gingie that it would be a good idea to comply. Vince didn't know about any of this, and Roe decided not to tell him. Vince was still mad at Roe for telling Gingie the truth about the surgery.

"What's *The Tempest*?" Whoofie asked, still frowning at the cards Milo had dealt her.

"I hate the beach," Milo grumbled. "Sand in everything."

"It's a play by Shakespeare," Roe answered, trying in vain to concentrate on his Le Carré novel.

"*William* Shakespeare?" Whoofie asked. "Milo, I don't think I have enough cards."

"This is Fizzbin, Whoofie, you only need four cards. Ante up." Having extracted some money from her, Milo continued, "My dear ignoramus, there is only one Shakespeare. *The Tempest is* about a sorcerer, Prospero —"

"No kidding! Like our Prospero?"

"Just like ours," Milo assured her blandly. "Having retreated from civilization after being ill-used, Prospero hides out on an island paradise. Very much like this one, in fact, only even *more* isolated, deserted, and dull."

"I like it here," the Doctor said.

"Then," Milo continued, "contrary to Prospero's wishes, his island starts filling up with people."

"Like us?" Whoofie asked.

"Just like us, Whoofie, dear, except that these people are shipwrecked. Well, to make a long story short, they wreak havoc on Prospero's sleepy little island and turn his life upside down." Milo added slyly, "And he just can't seem to get rid of them."

"How does it end?" Whoofie asked, looking up from her cards.

His gaze as rosily obscure as ever, Milo glanced toward Roe. "In the end, Prospero comes to his senses. He decides to return to civilization with them."

"You mean he goes back to New York?" Whoofie said, propping her chin on her hand.

"Something like that," Milo replied. "Raise, call, or fold?"

"I've never heard of Fizzbin, Milo," Roe said casually.

"You *have* been away a long time," Milo retorted.

"Wait a minute!" Whoofie threw down her cards and stared at Milo. "Are you pulling something here?"

"Only your leg, darling," Milo assured her. "The play actually ends with Prospero getting ensnared by a siren. A celibate one at that."

"Celibate?" Whoofie repeated blankly. "Oh, you mean famous."

"Precisely," Milo said dryly.

"Oh." After a doubtful moment, Whoofie said, "I think I'll go for a swim now."

"What do you think, Roe?" Milo asked, shuffling his cards. "Is fourteen years long enough to hide in the wilderness? Or thirty-four years, for that matter?"

"I haven't been hiding," Roe snapped.

"Haven't you?"

In a lower voice, Roe asked, "How do you know so much about Gingie?"

"About *you* and Gingie, don't you mean?" Milo smirked. "I can read her like a book. Apart from the fact that I've worked with her for twelve years, she's hardly what you'd call discreet. And you," Milo added, "are not as forbidding as you try to be. Any sensible man would have kicked us all off the island days ago, regardless of his brother's wishes"

Roe grunted and shifted uncomfortably. Seeing Milo's amusement, he added defensively, "I'm used to this. Having all of you here isn't that different from guiding a dozen Londoners through the bush for a month."

Milo sighed. "You might as well give in, Roe. I've known Gingie since she was nineteen, and I've never seen her behave like this before. Didn't you see the way she picked at her lunch yesterday?"

"Picked?" Roe repeated incredulously. "She ate as much as a college linebacker."

"Precisely! She usually eats as much as three longshoremen. She's melancholy when you're not with us and miserable when you are. Face facts, Prospero Hunter, you blew your last chance of having a peaceful life when you let Gingie fall for you."

"I *didn't* let . . . She hasn't really . . ." Giving up, Roe lay back on his blanket, covered his face with his book, and grumbled, "Don't talk to me any more today, Milo. You're depressing me."

"Too late, Roe," Milo said gleefully. "Look who's home."

Roe lifted the book away from his face long enough to see Gingie scramble down the last few stone steps to the beach and come racing across the sand. Having no idea what he should do or say, he covered his face again and lay like a rug.

"Roe!" Gingie cried. "I've just had the most wonderful idea!" She plopped down beside him and snatched the book off his face. So much for pretending to be asleep, he thought sourly.

"Hi, Gingie," Milo said.

"Hmm? Oh! Hi, Milo," she said distractedly, gazing at Roe with an intensity that made passion pool in his loins.

Her face was prettily flushed, and her pale blond hair was windblown beneath her straw hat. She was wearing an embroidered shawl draped around her hips like a skirt, and her slender legs were covered by paisley-patterned tights. She was also wearing a red halter top and a short denim jacket covered with patches from all over the world. She looked good enough to eat.

"How'd the interview go?" Roe asked, his mind a blank.

"Hmm? Oh! Fine." She kept staring at him, her eyes traveling down his bare chest and long, suntanned legs.

"What's your great idea, Gin?" Milo prodded while the Doctor sauntered past them to join Whoofie in the water.

"Hmm? Oh! I've decided how to help Santa Cecilia."

"Uh, she's been dead a long time, Gin," Milo said. "I think she's a little past help."

"No, you don't understand. After the interview, I took Casey — that's the journalist — to see the church. I thought maybe she could do a story about what a shame it is to see it falling into ruin. But she helped me come up with an even better idea. I told her I was so moved by the story you told me about Saint Cecilia, Roe, that I've nearly finished writing a song inspired by it."

"Really?" Roe sat up, interested now.

Gingie nodded. Milo added, "Yeah, she let me hear a little of it yesterday. It's good."

"So Casey suggested I release it as a single and make the fans aware that the profits will go directly into a restoration fund for Santa Cecilia."

"That's a good idea," Roe said, touched that she wanted to do something for the island and the people.

"And then, while Zu Aspanu was bringing me back, I realized that this is one of the most beautiful places I've ever seen," Gingie explained with growing excitement. "So why don't we also make a video for the song? Here! Now!"

"A video?" Roe repeated weakly. "Oh, Gingie —"

"I've got it all figured out," Gingie rushed on. "Naturally, we'll have to shoot some of the lip-sync close-ups in New York, since we can't record the song till we get back there. But there's so much we can do right here!"

"But Gingie —" Roe began.

"Your uncle was a cameraman in Hollywood, so I'm sure he can help out. And Gaspare can help, too." She glanced over to where the boy was sleeping in the sun. "He's very impassioned about video cameras and technical things like that."

"I don't think —"

"And you're here to organize it, Roe," Gingie concluded. "I've noticed that you're very good at organizing things."

"He was just saying how much dealing with us resembles his usual job," Milo chimed in.

"But that's —"

"I don't really understand these things," Gingie confessed, "but I suppose we'll need to get permission from the town council to film on the island. We'll obviously also need to talk to someone at Santa Cecilia. The priest, maybe? And we'll need to acquire the necessary equipment. There's bound to be paperwork, and —"

"Gingie, I don't want you to do this." Roe's statement fell like a lead balloon.

She squinted at him, as if uncertain she'd heard him correctly. "What?"

He spread his hands helplessly. "Look, I think your motives are very commendable, and recording the song is a great idea, but doing a video here on Sontara . . ." He shook his head.

"But why?" She looked so hurt he wanted to cut his own throat. Even more than that, he wanted to gather her into his arms and comfort her.

"Well, it's complicated, for one thing."

"But, Roe, I've *got* to do it. Don't you understand?"

"Gingie, I don't think you realize what an undertaking this would be," he protested.

"I've done lots of videos," she insisted hotly.

"But Vince organized the details and someone else produced them. You just . . ." He didn't realize what he was saying until it was too late to call back the words.

"All I had to do was sing and dance, like any dumb blond," she finished huffily.

"I didn't mean —"

"Yes, you did! My friend Luke Swain has raised hundreds of thousands for the homeless, but you don't think I'm capable of raising even enough to restore one little church!"

"I didn't say that."

"Oh, yes, you did!"

"I just meant that . . . Oh, hell."

"Please, Roe," she pleaded. "This is so important to me. I've *got* to do this. I've got to use my talent to help someone, instead of just providing an escape. And I've got to prove to myself that I can do something without Vince."

Roe blinked in surprise. She had talked about her frustration and dissatisfaction, but she had never before talked about cutting Vince out.

"I'm sorry," she murmured, seeing his expression. "But he's always made me feel like . . . like I can't do anything without him. He'll probably believe that forever, no matter what I do, but I can't stand another day of thinking it might be true."

He didn't like to think of how much more Sontara would change when one of the biggest names in pop music started filming a video there. But he found, to his surprise, that he couldn't deny Gingie an experience she needed so badly just because it would jeopardize his tranquillity, his haven, his final refuge. He realized, with a quiver of wariness, that she was rapidly destroying the carefully cultivated selfishness that had helped him survive.

"All right," he said in defeat. "Let's do it."

Gingie laughed with delight and threw her arms around him, tumbling down to the blanket with him. "I knew you'd help me!"

The sun-warmed scent of her flesh assaulted his senses, the soft mounds of her breasts pressed luxuriantly against his hard chest, and the sexual effervescence that so characterized Gingie ensnared him. Tenderness overwhelmed him, affection flooded through him, and the need to give her whatever she wanted — including enough space to spread her wings — took root in his heart.

He slid his palms under her denim jacket and caressed the silken skin of her back, left bare by her halter top. "It's just too hard to say no to you, Gingie," he admitted with a lazy smile.

"What'll we tell Vince, kids?" Milo asked, reminding them of his presence.

"Hmm? Oh!" Gingie sat up and straightened her jacket, blushing enchantingly. Roe folded his arms behind his head and watched her. "We'll . . . I'll . . . Um . . ."

"I'll handle Vince." When Gingie opened her mouth to protest, Roe added, "He's my brother. I know how to deal with him" He was relieved when she nodded her agreement. The news that Gingie was organizing and producing her own video would be enough of a strain on Vince's recovering heart, even without Gingie's somewhat incoherent way of approaching most conversations.

"This calls for a celebration," Milo said. "Why don't we all go out tonight?"

"Out? On Sontara?" Roe asked wryly.

"Well, we could dress up, try the other *trattoria,* and maybe talk Don Ciccio into giving us a joyride on his golf cart."

Roe smiled. "You guys go ahead. I'm going to stay home and enjoy the peace and quiet."

"But it won't be any fun without you," Gingie said ingenuously.

"Thanks a lot, Gin," Milo chided.

"I'm always with *you,* " she said by way of explanation.

"You need to get out for an evening," Milo shot back. "You're starting to look wan and peaked."

"Really?" She looked alarmed. "It must be because I haven't been drinking my daily infusion of raspberry leaves lately. I'd better go do that now." She hopped up and left them staring after her.

Finally, Milo said, "I'm telling you, Roe. Give in."

*D*ressed to kill in a little black number with gold beads and spaghetti straps, Gingie picked at the delicious meal which had been prepared by the chief competitors of Signora Gambarossa. Everyone from the villa, plus several other people, were at the long dinner table with her. Everyone except Roe, that is, and his absence made the whole evening seem hollow. Fortunately, Gingie was seated between Sandy and shy Maria, so at least she didn't have to talk much; silence always seemed to content both of them.

Roe's plan wasn't working so well, at least not from Gingie's point of view. She thought about him constantly, thought of the way he smiled when he was trying not to, the way his brown eyes gleamed gold when he was angry or passionate or amused, the way his muscles rippled with perfect definition under his suntanned, sweat-slick skin while he napped restlessly or worked with Gaspare under the blazing Silician sun.

Lying sleeplessly in her bed every night, she dreamed of him materializing in her room, sweeping her up in his brawny arms, and masterfully ending the torment of her gnawing indecision.

She had always been so sure of being on the right path. Could she have been wrong?

For years, she had thought of herself like a vestal virgin of some pagan cult, like a high priestess from some myth or legend, like Saint Cecilia, who had pledged her sensuality to a greater power than herself.

What had started out as common sense — refusing to sleep her way to the top or indulge in casual sex during all those lonely nights on the road — had become a superstition with her. She had channeled all her unused sexual energy into her work. She had gradually grown to believe that this was the very reason that she became known as the most vividly, alluringly, mysteriously sensual performer of her time. It was that very quality, more than any other, that had pushed her to the top of the most heartbreakingly competitive and cutthroat business in the world and had kept a fickle public coming back to her again and again.

As she grew older, the magic only grew stronger, and this confirmed her conviction that her life-style was the key ingredient to her extraordinary success. The one thing she had always cared about more than anything else was getting the whole world to listen to her songs.

What if she lost that special quality for which she was so famous? Would they still listen? Would she still be the best? Or would her gift dry up and wither? Would the muse of fire punish her for turning away from the melodies in her head to enjoy the pleasures granted to any ordinary woman?

"Gingie!" Milo shouted across the table. "You're falling behind! Have some more *involtini*. This stuff is great."

After a few more pokes at her food, Gingie dropped her fork dispiritedly. "It's hot in here," she said to Sandy. "I'm going for a walk. Tell everyone not to worry if I'm gone for a while." For once, Sandy didn't look panic-stricken about being left alone. In fact, his secretive smile puzzled her.

Gingie left the *trattoria* and wandered out into the starry night. The evenings on Sontara had so far been pleasantly cool, but she wasn't chilly tonight in her sleeveless dress. A warm wind had kicked up shortly before sundown, turning the air soft and balmy. Roe had told her this wind came from the Sahara and was called *scirocco*. He made even the wind sound romantic.

She sighed. What did Roe want? she wondered. She had seen desire in his eyes more than once, but there was also a wariness that often came upon him without warning. He was so intelligent and experienced, he understood so many things. Could a man like him really care about someone as basically stupid and naïve as she was?

Gingie tilted her head back and looked up toward the towering, ancient church spire, outlined against the night sky by the light of the waning moon. "Santa Cecilia," she whispered. "I'm helping you, so please help me. What should I do?"

There was no answer, and Gingie realized that this decision was too important to trust to anyone else, anyhow.

In the end, she decided upon the only solution possible. This thing between her and Roe was eating away at her, dostroying her concentration, obliterating her self-discipline, and draining all her energy. Not to mention her appetite.

This spring had become her season of change, and she was about to take the biggest step of all. After pacing the streets of the village for half an hour, Gingie finally returned to the *trattoria* and, without asking, took Gaspare's bicycle. He could go home in the donkey cart with Zu Aspanu. She knew the boy wouldn't worry about the missing bike. Aside from the fact that there was no theft on Sontara, Gingie was pretty sure Milo would immediately guess what had happened and provide a convenient excuse to Gaspare.

*R*oe stood on the terrace outside the house and watched the light of the waning moon as it flirted with the sea. For days now, he had repeatedly wished for a few hours alone in his house. Now that he had them, he couldn't relax. He missed Gingie. This was the first time in years that he had been anything but grateful for a little solitude.

Confirming his growing suspicion that he was hopelessly masochistic, at least in the matter of his unfulfilled passion for a radical celibate, he turned on the tape player. Gingie's voice flooded the night, teasing, promising, pleading. *Make Me Forget Him* had made the top forty when it was released, and every man in America must have wanted to answer the beckoning throb of Gingie's voice when they heard that song. It was followed by *When the Cat's Away*, a sexy, playful song of fast, clever lyrics and an extraordinarily complex melody. Gingie was halfway through *Last Night in Rio* when the tape deck suddenly clicked off.

Roe whirled around to find Gingie herself standing next to it. She shrugged. "Being on vacation with Whoofie is almost like being on tour. I'm sick of the sound of my own voice."

Her short, gold-beaded black dress made her seem like a dizzying combination of a sailor's fantasy and a *contessa*. His chest felt tight, and so did another part of his body. "Where's everyone else?"

"Having dinner. I wasn't hungry." She walked over to join him at the railing.

Her statement brought a smile of amusement to his face. "*You* weren't hungry? What is it — plague or cholera?"

She frowned at the sea. "I think it's you."

His blood flashed hotly through his veins and his belly tensed. "Didn't anyone ever teach you that it's not always wise to tell the truth?"

"Didn't anyone ever teach you that the truth is our only protection?"

she shot back.

"You say the damnedest things," he muttered. How had any of them ever mistaken her for just a sexy, silly blond?

"With all the crazy things that people say and write about me, my only safety is in always knowing and telling the truth," she said in a low, pensive voice.

Roe stared out at the sea, too, every cell of his body burningly aware of her. "Gingie, we agreed . . . I mean, what are you doing here alone? And in that dress?"

A balmy breeze brushed Gingie's yellow curls, carrying the scents of wisteria and jasmine, lemon groves and wild rosemary. The leaves rustled softly ail around them, whispering to them.

"I've come to sacrifice a virgin," she said at last.

He drew in a sharp breath, which she hoped was a good sign. "I think you've come to sacrifice my sanity."

"I can't think about anything else, Roe." She turned to face him, her heart swelling at the way the moonlight highlighted his raven-black hair, at the way he held himself rigid and taut, as if he expected her to attack him. "It's never been like this for me before. No one's ever made me feel the way you do." When he didn't respond, she rushed on, "I'm overheated and shaky all the time, melancholy and distracted, sad and happy all at once. I feel as hungry as if I were starving, but food just gets stuck in my throat. I think about you all night long, about touching you, about the way you touched me that day —"

"Stop it!"

She blinked in surprise. His voice was rough and desperate, as if she had hurt him. "I can't," she said honestly.

His hands had a death grip on the railing, and his arms were braced like steel. His breath started coming faster. "You'd better go inside."

"No! I told you. I've made up my mind." She licked her lips. "I want you. That's why I'm here." When he didn't respond, she asked, "Don't you want me, Roe?"

When he looked away, pain and humiliation washed over her. He didn't want her. She had crossed the Rubicon, she was ready to burn her bridges, she was ready to risk the wrath of her muse for him, and he was rejecting her.

"Well, I guess I was wrong." Her voice was husky and tremulous. She took a deep breath, using all her experience to control it. "I thought you'd be glad. I thought this was what you wanted, too. But I should have known that someone like you would never want to get tangled up with someone like me."

Still looking away, he said, "Gingie, I don't know if I can make you understand."

"No, you probably can't," she replied, her voice cracking despite her efforts to control it. "Everyone knows that I don't understand anything except music. I'm stupid and naïve. My work is all I know. A man like you must be bored to death with me. I'm —"

"Bored?" he repeated incredulously. "Did you say *bored?*" He faced her at last, his expression almost outraged.

Her eyes misted, humiliating her in front of him. "You must think I'm so foolish and ignorant, such a burden and so . . ."

"Gingie, don't," he said gruffly, inching closer to her.

Hurt welled up uncontrollably. "Thirty-one years!" she hurled at him. "And the first time I want to . . . The first man I've ever really . . ." She swallowed a sob and continued, "And I'm skinny and my hips are too wide —"

"*What?*"

She was crying now, mortified but unable to stop. "And I'm . . . I'm white as a dead fish!"

"Oh, Gingie, Gingie." A moment later she was in his arms, her head pillowed on his broad, warm chest. He stroked her hair gently and kissed her temple. "Is that really what you think?"

She sniffed and choked, "Sometimes."

He hugged her more tightly to him. "I don't know where you got any of those crazy ideas." Rubbing his hand over her firm bottom, he pressed their hips snugly together. "Feel that?"

She gasped in surprise. "Um, yes."

"My pants caught fire the day we met, and they haven't cooled off since. You are the sexiest, loveliest, most tempting woman I've ever met. *That's* the problem, Gingie. Do you think I'd be so moody if it wasn't taking all my strength just to keep my hands off you?"

She tilted her head back to look up at him. "But why? You don't have to, now."

He sighed her name and touched her cheek. "You're not the only one who's been lying awake wondering what it would be like between us," he assured her.

"Then don't be so noble," she urged. "Stop taxing your strength. Take me somewhere with a door we can lock."

Their eyes held for a moment, then he lowered his head to hers. "Why can't I ever refuse you anything?" he murmured a moment before their mouths met, melded, and clung.

His lips were warm and moist, tender and pliant, rubbing against hers so thoroughly that she sagged breathlessly against him, her senses spinning, her strength ebbing away. She kissed him back with more enthusiasm than expertise, delighting in the groan that rippled through him and the way his arms tightened reflexively around her. She brushed her fingers through the dark silk of his hair and nuzzled his cheek and jaw affectionately, inhaling his musky male scent as it mingled with the night's heady perfume.

"Not here," he whispered at last. "The cottage."

"Hmm? Oh!" He was right, she realized. They had no way of knowing when the others would decide to come home. She gasped a moment later when he scooped her up in his arms and started carrying her down the tree-lined path to the guest house.

"Did you say 'skinny,' woman?" he asked breathlessly.

"I know I'm heavy," she said guiltily. "It's because I'm so tall. You can put me down if you —"

"No, I need the exercise," he teased. He gave her an experimental squeeze. "Anyhow, you've got padding in all the right places. And I suspect that twenty million men in America agree with me."

"But that's different," she explained. "That's . . . my job. It's not as if those people *know* me." She shrugged when he gave her a puzzled look. "They just automatically associate a lot of glamour with a rock star, but that doesn't have anything to do with reality."

"You're a beautiful woman," he insisted. "On or off stage. I thought you knew that." When she didn't answer, he prodded, "Gingie? Why don't you think so? What's all this about being white as a dead fish and —"

"Well, I am."

"Open the door," he instructed when they reached the cottage. She reached out to turn the knob. He carried her across the threshold and kicked the door shut behind them. The interior was simple, a spacious bedroom and sitting room with a few pieces of sturdy, wooden furniture. Moonlight flooded the room through an open seaward window, spilling brightly across the massive bed.

"Um . . ." Gingie said as Roe let her feet slide to the floor.

He stilled. "Second thoughts?" he asked.

"No," she answered hesitantly.

"Then what?" he whispered, pulling her body firmly against him. "Nerves?"

"I think so," she admitted.

"Then I'll have to see what I can do about that." He grinned, that teasing, wicked, slightly dangerous grin that always made her heart skip a beat. He stroked her hair and added tenderly, "I'll try to be gentle, but sometimes the first time hurts, Gingie."

"I know that."

His fingers brushed her throat. "Oh? How do *you* know so much?" he murmured against her temple.

"I'm inexperienced, but I'm not totally naïve, Roe," she said primly. "Haven't you heard my songs?"

"Yeah," he breathed, pushing her straps down her shoulders. "That's why your little revelation was such a shock."

His hard palms lightly caressed her bare shoulders, their warm touch dizzying and erotic. He lowered his head, and his lips were hot against her bare skin, slow and sultry and thorough.

"I've been wondering," he asked, gently nipping her ear.

"What?"

"Well, I don't want to sound crass, but . . . how the hell can you still be a virgin? Why didn't some kid show you the back seat of his car fifteen years ago? That's what I'd have done if I'd known you then."

"No, you wouldn't," she said flatly.

"Oh, honey, I sure would. I've learned a little restraint over the years, but back then I took whatever I wanted."

"You wouldn't have wanted me."

He lifted his head and met her gaze in the shadows. He realized that she was completely serious. His hands continued to stroke and explore the delicious softness of her skin as he asked, "Why do you say that?"

She pressed closer to him, snuggling into his arms and hiding her face against his shoulder, as if she were ashamed. "Oh, Roe, I was an incredibly unattractive teenager."

"Sure, all teenagers are a little odd, but —"

"No, you don't understand." Her voice was slightly muffled. "I was skinny as a rail, and gawky and clumsy. I didn't start filling out till I was eighteen. All the other girls had beautiful summer tans, and I was white as a —"

"Some kid said that to you?" he whispered, recognizing the hurt in her voice. When she nodded, he rubbed her back, wishing he could take away all her pain. Who'd have thought that Gingie still thought of herself as a homely, gawky teenage girl?

"And I had dull, limp, plain, stringy, mousy-brown hair, and no one ever *looked* at me," she continued, her hands curling into fists on his shoulders. "So, you see, you wouldn't have looked at me, either, fifteen years ago."

He supposed she was right. At nineteen, he had been at the all-time low point of his life. Between the intoxicants that ran through his bloodstream and the women who ran through his bedroom, he would never have had the time, sense, or sensitivity to notice a gawky teenage girl whose astonishing beauty and stupendous talent were still raw and undirected.

"I look at you now," he assured her, glad she hadn't known that confused nineteen-year-old. "I look at you all of the time, even when you think I'm not looking. I haven't been able to take my eyes off you since you got here."

"Really?" She finally lifted her head from his shoulder and met his gaze again.

"Really." He touched her yellow hair. "So it's not your natural color?"

When she shook her head, he added, "It should be. It suits you perfectly. When did you choose it?"

"About eight years ago. I tried some other colors before that. Red, black, pink, green —"

"What?"

"Those were the days of punk," she explained. "I guess you missed all that, out in the bush."

"I remember some of it. I'm just trying to picture you with pink-and-green hair," he said dryly.

"Vince begged me to change it for nearly a year before I finally gave in. Everyone but him liked it. Even my mother."

Roe kissed her lightly on the mouth and squeezed her bottom experimentally. "Everything else feels pretty real to me."

"It is." She frowned a moment later. "Except my eyebrows and eyelashes. I have them dyed black." She laughed a moment later. "You should see your face!"

"You have your eyelashes *dyed?*" he repeated incredulously. "Does it hurt?"

She laughed again. "No, of course not. I guess your mother was so beautiful she didn't have to have secrets."

"Not those kind of secrets, I suppose, but she had plenty of secrets, Gingie. Anyhow, the end result is what matters. And *this* end result," he said, kissing her cheek, her eyelids, her hair, and her temple, "is well worth the effort."

"Do you really think so?" she asked uncertainly. "Looking good on stage or for the camera is one thing. But looking good for you is . . . different."

"You always look good to me," he insisted. "And your skin," he continued, touching her shoulders, neck, and arms with long, hungry caresses, "is like moonlight, mother of pearl, alabaster. You're so soft that I . . ." He lost track of what he was saying. His body stirred almost painfully, and his breathing quickened. Wanting her to believe what he already knew, he said, "Everything's going to be all right, Gingie. It's going to be very, very good between us. Trust me."

"I do," she whispered, "or I wouldn't be here. I wouldn't have told you all that."

"I'm glad you told me," he murmured. "I don't want you to be nervous." He reached behind her and began slowly pulling down her zipper. "I want you to know how beautiful you are."

"You make me feel beautiful." Her eyes grew heavy-lidded, and her hands moved restlessly over his chest, exciting him with their eager, unpracticed exploration.

"Unbutton my shirt," he urged softly.

Gingie did as he asked, distracted by the warmth of his palms on her back, the hot touch of his lips on her mouth, her face, her shoulders, and the insistent pressure of his hips against hers. She suddenly realized that if she had known him fifteen years ago, as underconfident as she was at the time, she probably would have thrown herself at him anyhow. She had kept her head all these years, devoted herself entirely to her work, and resisted the advances of some of the most sought-after men in the world without much real effort, but only because she hadn't known Roe.

When she had finally finished unbuttoning his shirt, he shrugged out of it. Then he peeled down her dress until it pooled at her feet, leaving her wearing only her lacy black panties, garter belt, stockings, and gold-studded pumps.

"What did I tell you?" he breathed. *"Beautiful."*

He cupped her breasts in his palms and squeezed gently. She moaned, and he massaged the soft mounds tenderly, whispering dark, exciting things to her. Her nipples hardened to painfully sensitive buds under the friction of his calloused fingertips, and she started trembling uncontrollably.

He pulled her roughly against him, his kiss deep, his tongue velvety and searching, his arms unyielding, and his chest wonderfully warm and abrasive. Her eyes flew open when he picked her up and strode toward the bed with her.

"There's the altar," he rasped. "Let's sacrifice a virgin."

Nine

*T*hey sank together to the sun-smelling, moon-streaked sheets, their bodies twining together, their hands restless, their mouths hungry and demanding. His kisses completely destroyed the breath control she had spent nearly twenty years perfecting, and the shameless touch of his hands made her whimper in a strained, high-pitched voice.

"Oof! Gingie, you shouldn't wear your shoes to bed," he teased when she accidentally kicked him. He sat up and, smiling at her, removed her expensive shoes one by one. "While we're at it . . ." He smoothed his hand up the length of her calf, squeezing it affectionately, then ran it along the inside of her thigh with agonizing slowness. Gingie bit her lip, her breasts heaving up and down as she watched him. A moment later he slid his fingers into the lacy hem of her panties and started pulling them down.

She watched him slide them slowly, smoothly down her thighs, over her knees, and past her calves and ankles. He held them up to admire them for a moment, then dropped them to the floor.

"What about my stockings?" she whispered a moment later.

"Don't take them off just yet. They turn me on." He winked at her, making her laugh.

"Shouldn't *you* take something off?" she prodded.

He kissed her again, then slid off the bed and unbuckled his belt. She sat up and watched in fascination as he unsnapped and unzipped his jeans, then pushed them off, along with his briefs. His shoulders loomed broad and hard in the moonlight, his legs were long and muscular, and a thin line of black hair trailed from his chest, down his stomach, to his groin, where he had a tan line. Gingie's gaze became riveted on that particular part of his magnificent body.

"It . . . sort of has a life of its own, doesn't it?" she asked as casually as possible.

He smiled. "It doesn't always do what I tell it to," he admitted. "Especially around you"

"Is it . . . very uncomfortable right now?"

"Yes." He sat down beside her. "But you'll take care of that."

"I will?" she asked doubtfully.

"Oh, yeah." He slid his hand over her stomach and let it rest low on her abdomen. "And I'll take care of your ache."

"Oh, good," she sighed. "It's been there for days and days, and you've just made it a lot worse."

"It hurts here?" he asked, sliding his fingers across her flat belly.

"Yes."

"And here?" He slid them a little lower.

"Oh, yes."

"And here?" He cupped his hand over her soft mound.

"Oh . . ." She drew an unsteady breath. "Yes. A whole lot."

"I'll bet it hurts there, too," he whispered, sliding his fingers into the hot, wet, waiting petals of feminine flesh.

"Oh! Ohhhh . . ." She wanted to tell him how good it suddenly felt at the same time that it still hurt, but she could find no words, despite the long, low sounds that spilled involuntarily from her lips.

He lay across her, his weight pressing her into the mattress, and greedily kissed the swell of one breast, then the other, as they rose and fell with her labored breathing. "Still hurts?" he mumbled, his fingers exploring her boldly, obliterating her modesty, inflaming her senses. Her hands clutched his shoulders, tangled in his hair, moved restlessly over the smooth skin of his back, eager to touch him, hungry for something more.

He licked her nipple, whispering to her when she gasped in surprise, then licked it again, tormenting her with his satiny tongue, circling the aching peak over and over. Then he nipped her gently, several times, and the tickling, almost painful nibbling of his white teeth made her arch toward him.

"What about this?" he asked silkily. "Does it hurt, too?"

When his clever fingers found the ultra-sensitive bud hidden in the slick, swollen, achingly tender place between her thighs, she nearly jumped out of her skin.

"Easy, easy," he murmured.

"Oh, God," she moaned, clinging to him. "Is it supposed to feel like that?"

"How does it feel?"

"Like I'm dying," she panted. "Like you're killing me. Like my heart's going to burst."

"Do you want me to stop?"

"No! No, then I'll die for sure."

He kissed her cheek, her mouth, her breast. "That's *exactly* how it's supposed to feel, honey."

His fingers continued their delicate dance between her legs, moving faster and then, when she felt near to weeping, moving more slowly to let her catch her breath. She kissed him fervently, caressing his tongue with hers, loving his agile, velvety invasion of her mouth. She sighed when he lowered his head, then arched her back off the bed when he closed his mouth around one nipple and sucked, gently at first, then with increasing force as her reaction assured him she liked it. She stroked his hair and his neck, feeling as if he were drawing her soul out of her body.

When he finally stopped, he was breathing so hard that his breath rasped hotly across her stomach, burning it as he rested his head there. "This hurts, too," he murmured, taking her hand and drawing it down his body. He wrapped her fingers around the hot shaft that moved restlessly between them, showing her how he liked to be touched. "It hurts so much."

"I want to make the pain stop," she told him, hoping her inexperienced caresses incited him the way his inflamed her.

He closed his eyes. "That's helping . . ." A moment later he drew a sharp breath and started shaking. "No, that's making it worse. A whole lot worse. Oh, Gingie, did you just make that up? Honey, stop, before I . . ." He gritted his teeth. "Oh, that's *good.*" Breathing like he'd just run twenty miles, he slid his hand farther down.

"What are you doing?" she could barely force the words out.

"Just seeing how you're made," he murmured. He slipped a finger inside her and added, "Very tightly."

"Is that bad?"

He almost laughed, but the way she unconsciously squeezed him when she asked the question made him shudder with the effort not to turn her first time into a sudden disappointment. "No, it's not bad," he assured her, reluctantly but firmly removing her hand. "We're going to fit perfectly."

"Are you sure?" she asked doubtfully. The first flash of fear entered her expression as she glanced down at his body.

"I'm sure," he promised her, pushing a second finger inside her and moving his palm massagingly, trying to relax her. "Just tell me if it hurts, and we'll . . ." He paused, since he didn't know what they'd do. They sure as hell weren't going to stop. "We'll work it out," he concluded.

He shifted, covering her with his body, and she clasped his hips instinctively with her legs. He felt her black stockings against his skin, and his blood roared in his ears. He braced one arm beside her and used the other to lead her hand down between their bodies. "You help me find what's comfortable for you."

Gingie looked into his impassioned, gold-flecked eyes and nodded trustingly. She felt another instinctive flash of fear at his first probing touch, but she kept her gaze locked with his, and the tenderness in his expression quickly banished her moment of panic.

Arching gracefully above her, he found the hot entrance to her body and pushed slowly inside her. A moment later her hand moved to his hip, and his slid underneath her bottom, lifting her to him. Gingie squeezed her eyes shut and swallowed a gasp as he thrust deeper, moving slowly, his face contorted with the effort of his self-control, his forehead beaded with sweat.

Tight. It was so tight, and a little uncomfortable, and amazingly wonderful. She made a brief, harsh sound as he pulled her hips off the bed and thrust twice, then again, harder. His head lolled forward with relief, and he whispered, "What did I tell you? A perfect fit."

"It feels a little tight," she mumbled, her chest aching with her excitement.

"Did I hurt you?"

"Not really. I thought — *Oh.*" Her voice caught in her throat as he pulled halfway out of her and thrust again. And again.

They moved slowly at first, his hands guiding her hips, then faster, their sweat-slick bodies gliding rhythmically together and apart, their harsh breath and rapturous sighs blending with the soft squeaking of Roe's ancient bed and the muffled thud of the headboard against the plaster wall. Gingie lifted her knees higher, trying to pull him deeper, deeper still.

The climax started in that aching part of her body that welcomed him so snugly, so hotly, then it flooded through the rest of her, scorching her veins, filling her breasts, pouring through her stomach and limbs with trembling, soaring pleasure, with wave after wave of shattering fulfillment, engulfing her in a bonfire of delight. He continued to thrust into her again and again, his lips branding her neck and shoulders, his hands finding ways to increase and extend the pleasure, until she was sobbing with feelings that couldn't be contained.

She went limp at last and lay there, her breath shallow and uneven, her skin flushed and damp, her body quaking in the aftermath of something so glorious.

"Oh, Roe," she sighed. She opened her eyes to find him watching her, his eyes aglow, his face dark with tension. "Is it always like this?"

"No," he murmured. "No. This is . . . the best."

He was shaking, his hips shifting restlessly, his hardness stirring hungrily inside her. She asked, "Don't you want to . . ."

"Oh, yeah, I definitely do. But I wanted to watch you."

"You watched?"

"Don't be embarrassed," he coaxed, pressing quick, hard kisses to her mouth. "I wanted to. It's . . . exciting. Erotic." His lips drifted over her cheeks. "You're lovely, moving beneath me, crying out, clinging to me." He smiled slightly. "And you're even graceful in the middle of a climax."

"Now you're teasing me."

"No. *This,*" he said, drawing back until he had almost left her, "is teasing you." He plunged into her again, and she felt only pleasure this time. He kissed her deeply, then pulled all the way out of her. She whimpered when he rubbed the hard tip of his manhood against the sensitive place that had already responded to his hands.

With that slow, breath-stealing grin, he levered himself off her and rose to his knees. "I want to feel your bare legs wrapped around me this time," he said, his voice low and gravelly. He removed her garters first with unsteady hands, then peeled her stockings off her legs while she watched, propped up on her elbows. He removed the first one slowly, kissing her thigh, her knee, her calf, and her ankle as he went. The second stocking, however, he slid impatiently down her leg and tossed over his shoulder.

Then he pulled her off the pillows and lifted her so she straddled him. As their mouths locked together in a long, wet kiss, Roe guided Gingie's hips as she lowered herself onto him.

He sank all the way inside her, then groaned and buried his face against her neck, holding her so tightly she could scarcely breathe. Unwilling to wait, she moved against him, pushing herself up, sinking back down, then giving a little circular twist that she sensed would drive him wild.

It did, and suddenly he was thrusting strongly into her, the muscles of his back rippling with magnificent animal strength as he plunged into her again and again. He lowered his head and moved his mouth greedily over her breasts, suckling, nibbling, tugging strongly, pulling his arms even more tightly around her waist, encouraging her to arch into him even more as they rocked together in a primitive, ageless mating dance.

When she thought she couldn't draw another breath into her burning lungs, when she thought the protesting springs of the bed couldn't bear another moment of this pounding punishment, Gingie heard Roe growl, "Stay with me."

She felt him slide his hand between their bodies, then her senses exploded. He went rigid as he gave one last forceful thrust, every muscle in his body taut and ready to spring. Then he groaned, a long, low, intensely satisfied sound, and shook violently. A few moments later he sank to the mattress with her, and they lay side by side, their arms and legs tangled, their breath desperate and painful, their bodies sated and tingling.

"Oh, Roe," Gingie sighed.

He kissed her throat, her soft shoulder, the scented hollow behind her ear. "It's never been like that before," he admitted, his voice blurry and exhausted. "It's never been so . . . I wouldn't have noticed if a cannon had gone off ten feet away."

She nestled against him, drained of all energy, contented in a way she'd never known. "I'd give up singing," she sighed.

"What?" He frowned in puzzlement and, with his last bit of strength, turned his head to see her face.

She had already fallen asleep. He watched her for a moment, his chest filling with an almost painful sensation of tenderness. He smiled to himself, thinking he may well have created a monster. For all her inexperience, she had done more things to drive him crazy tonight than he had thought were possible. He couldn't even imagine what she'd be like a week from now.

Exhausted from his many restless nights, as well as from the past couple of hours, Roe laid his cheek against Gingie's hair and closed his eyes, figuring he'd better rest up for the future.

"*A*ren't you hungry?" Gingie prodded late the next morning. "I'm starved!"

"Naturally." He lay flat on his back, eyes closed, more exhausted and yet more content that he'd ever been in his life. "I don't think I have the strength to lift a fork."

She laughed and snuggled against him, pulling the thin cotton sheet over their bodies. They had made love again in the middle of the night, and then once more this morning. Gingie had never felt so wonderful. "I'll make you an herbal infusion later. It'll help you get your strength back"

Eyes still closed, he caressed one soft shoulder and kissed her tousled hair. "I have a feeling I'll need it."

"You look so relaxed," she murmured. She had never seen his face so smooth, so free of care and strain. "This is obviously good for you."

"Hmm. You're good for me," he corrected mildly.

"I'm glad." She rolled her head on his shoulder. "I thought . . . I don't know what I thought."

"You thought I'd be bored," he reminded her lazily, still amazed by that.

"Well . . . You might be," she said softly.

That made him open his eyes. She looked angelic and naughty at the same time, blooming with good health and vibrant energy, despite getting barely three or four hours sleep all night. She also looked slightly uncertain. "Gingie, I'd have to be a corpse to be bored around you," he assured her.

She shrugged. "You know so much about so many things, and I'm not very bright. I'm . . . ignorant."

"No, you're not." He frowned slightly. "How can you possibly think that?"

"Well, I am." She sat up and looked down at him, the sheet wrapped around her, its whiteness making the rich blue of her eyes even more vivid.

"Come on, I saw you reading those highbrow books," he began.

"You mean about sexual oppression and moldy bones in Anatolia?" When he nodded, she said, "I have to read those, Roe, my parents wrote them."

"Oh." He was getting the picture at last. "I see."

She sighed dispiritedly. "My parents are both brilliant scholars. My sister Letitia finished in the top five percent at medical school, and now she's becoming one of the most prominent homeopaths in New York. Camilla's got two doctorates and teaches at Columbia — when she's not busy with activism, I mean. All of those arrests kind of cut into her teaching schedule last year."

"I can just imagine," Roe said dryly.

"But I always got lousy grades and never retained anything. I had to take world history three times before my guidance counselor advised me to throw in the towel."

"And you were the youngest, so all your teachers expected you to be as good in school as Camilla and Letitia." When she nodded, he asked carefully, "What did your parents expect?"

"Well, my mother doesn't believe in imposing parental expectations or limitations on children. She and my father believe that child-rearing should be approached as an exercise in imparting moral decision-making capabilities, so we never really talked much about my grades." She looked down at her folded hands. "Of course, they were all so accomplished, I think they were concerned about my problems. When it was ascertained that I didn't have a learning disability, they couldn't understand why I still did so badly in school."

"You can follow that line of reasoning, which leaves me baffled, but you think you're dumb?" Smiling ruefully, Roe used the last of his strength to sit up and hug her. "It's just a different kind of intelligence, Gingie, that's all."

"I was even tested for learning disabilities," she admitted in remembered humiliation. With her head on his shoulder, she whispered, "I knew I was strange. I couldn't hear the teachers or understand the books because I heard music in my head, all of the time. Melodies, day and night. Rhythms and harmonies and lyrics."

"When did it become apparent you were gifted?" he asked. Her talent was so inherent, it must have blossomed when she was very young.

She slid her palm down his ribs, exploring the firm warmth of his body, wondering at the way the pain of being different and lonely for so many years was starting to recede. "I played the piano and the guitar as a kid, but it was when my voice changed that I found my niche. I was about twelve. Then I started singing, and I've never stopped. I wasn't any good at school or sports, and I wasn't pretty." She closed her eyes, remembering. "But I knew that no one could sing like I could."

"Were your parents interested?" he asked, stroking her hair.

"They were pleased I was so involved in something positive but they didn't understand. They still don't, but they listen to all my albums, which is why I feel I should read their books. Their love was unconditional, Roe, they just never knew what to make of me. It's as if they found me under a cabbage leaf."

He pulled back to meet her gaze. "It's often that way with truly gifted people," he assured her. "My mother always felt different, alone, outside. Her family loved her, but there was a gulf between them that could never be crossed. The farmers and shepherds she was born among couldn't understand her passion for her craft anymore than the intellectuals in your life can understand the melodies that echo in your head day and night."

"But you understand, don't you?" Gingie asked slowly, her heart flooding with recognition. "Maybe because *she* raised you. You know how it is for someone like me. Don't you?"

"Maybe" His expression clouded. "Maybe I just understand that those gifts need a lot of room, and they don't leave much space for the qualities that could balance them. Maybe they're too big to be balanced."

"So . . . you don't think it matters that much that I'm not very smart?" Her heart pounded, waiting for him to help her shift the weight of an age-old disappointment from her shoulders.

"Oh, Gingie, I think you're brilliant. That's what I've been telling you."

She slid her arms around him and pressed close. "Thank you." It was like a gift.

The tenderness swelling inside him caused something else to start swelling. Just before he gave into it, a chilling realization struck him.

"Oh, Roe," Gingie sighed, feeling him stir against her.

"Gingie," he said hoarsely, "we can't do this. Not right now, I mean."

"Why?" she asked lazily, rubbing against him in a way that made his mind go foggy.

"I don't want to get you pregnant." He felt her go still. "I know this is like shutting the barn door too late . . ."

Her jaw dropped as she looked at him. "I didn't even think of that. What did I just tell you? I'm so stupid!"

"Don't, Gingie," he pleaded. "I'm the experienced one, here. I should have —"

"My mother and my sisters would be so —"

"Shh." He hugged her to him. "I'll go to the *farmacia* and get some condoms, okay?" And he'd warn the *farmacista* not to gossip, though it might not do any good; the man was Signora Gamborossa's cousin. Roe nipped Gingie's earlobe and added teasingly, "Will three or four dozen hold us for the rest of the week?"

"Oh, Roe, I'm sorry." Her hand drifted down and closed gently on him. "I wish . . . I really want to . . ."

"So do I," he admitted, wondering where he got all this energy. He should be comatose by now. After they spent a few minutes playing with fire and teasing each other shamelessly, he pressed her into the pillows and whispered, "On second thought, I'll go to the pharmacy later."

"But what about —"

"Don't worry. There are a lot of ways we can have fun without risking getting you pregnant."

Gingie's eyes widened when he demonstrated. "Oh! *Oh, good.*"

"Well, kids, I was going to start taking bets on whether you were *ever* coming out of that cottage," Milo said dryly when Gingie and Roe appeared on the terrace toward noon.

"Is there any breakfast left? I'm hungry" Gingie said.

"Naturally," Milo said. He grinned at Roe. "Vince called."

"What about?" Roe asked warily.

"You were right. Those guys moored off the beach *were* photographers. There's a big story breaking in supermarkets across the US. about how Gmgie is shacked up in Sicily with you, me, and Sandy."

Roe groaned. Apparently unconcerned, Gingie seized a leftover croissant with delight and smeared it with jam. "Aren't you hungry, Roe?" she prodded.

"That's not all," Milo continued. "Sandy's manager is blaming Vince for Sandy's disappearance. Vince, of course, blamed me, and I wisely blamed Gingie. In fact, Sandy is about the only person who's *not* being blamed for his behavior. The upshot, Roe, is that you're supposed to convince him to go home immediately to fulfill his professional obligations."

"Me?" Roe asked, accepting the glass of juice Gingie was forcing upon him. "Why me? The kid hasn't spoken more than a dozen words to me since he got here. Gingie, you're going to have to talk to him."

"Where is he?" she asked Milo.

Milo shrugged. "I haven't seen him since last night. He walked Maria home and got back late."

"He walked Maria home?" Roe repeated. "Why? Is he worried about our escalating crime rate or something?"

"Sandy's very gentlemanly," Gingie explained.

"Anyhow, he was already gone when I got up this morning," Milo concluded. "But Roe's right, Gingie. Vince will have to go back into intensive care if we don't get Sandy back to New York soon."

"I'll talk to him," she promised. "He might be ready. Have you noticed that he's been less dependent for the past couple of days?"

"I'll call Vince and tell him not to worry about the tabloids," Roe said wearily. "You'd think he'd have gotten used to this by now."

"Are you going to tell him about the video we're making?" Gingie asked.

Roe nodded. He covered her hand with his. "I'll handle it. I have to go into town first. What are you going to do today?"

"Get some more food," she said with a frown. "Then I'm going to see if I can still sing."

"What?"

She kissed his cheek and went into the house, saying, "I'll explain later."

*T*he next two weeks were perhaps the most exciting in Gingie's life, which was saying a lot. Roe took her with him to meet with the priest at Santa Cecilia, then to a special town meeting, which was scheduled three days later. He gained popular support from the whole island for Gingie's endeavor and made her feel that her contributions were important during these initial planning stages. He raised her self-esteem in ways she had never realized it was deficient whenever he asked her opinion, translated a business discussion for her, or patiently explained things three and four times to make her understand.

Far from being punished by her muse for seeking earthly pleasures, Gingie's music caught fire, melodies flowing out of her head and into her voice even more richly and mysteriously than before. By the time she finished working on the song for the video, she thought it might be her best ever.

Sexual involvement with a man was distracting, as she had always feared it would be, but somehow that didn't seem like a detriment anymore. The nights were lost, as far as work went, since as soon as the door to Roe's cottage closed behind them, she heard no music except his sighs and groans, sensed no beat except the cadence of his breath, felt no rhythm except the exquisite one they made together as their bodies joined, frantically or leisurely, forcefully or tenderly, in the privacy of his bedroom.

And it wasn't only the nights that she lost from her schedule. She was getting out of bed later than she ever had in her life, and not regretting it for a moment. The first hours of each day were suddenly too precious to be shared with anyone but Roe. Gingie was equally thankful for the quiet afternoon siestas, when she and Roe would disappear together, whether to make love in the cottage, rest peacefully in the shadowed hammock, or talk privately as he lay on the sun-drenched beach and she sat next to him, wearing her big straw hat.

The way they worked together was also deeply satisfying to Gingie. Roe had spent years organizing people, equipment, schedules, and bureaucracy in Africa, so he organized the filming of a video on Sontara even more smoothly than she had expected. He admitted to her that Vince had expressed mixed feelings about the endeavor but Roe chose not to give her details of his conversations with his brother. They were relying on Vince to arrange packaging and distribution of the video and the record in Europe and America, since this was an area in which Roe had no experience.

He could learn quickly, though, Gingie thought. She said nothing, however, since it seemed inappropriate to ask him to usurp his brother's place. Furthermore, he already had a career.

Even more satisfying than their working relationship, however, and even more intimately binding than the sex, was their pillow talk. As they snuggled together in his bed or relaxed together in the shade, she told him more about herself than she'd ever told anyone. And as vague as he could be at times, she began to believe that she was learning more about him than he had ever permitted anyone else to.

"When are you going back to Africa?" she asked him one night, breaking the contented silence with the question that had plagued her for days.

After a long pause, he admitted, "I'm not. Not soon, anyhow."

Trying not to be too obvious about her relief, she prodded, "Why not? What do you mean? I thought this was your vacation."

"Not exactly. It's kind of complicated. My company's calling this an indefinite leave of absence."

"Are you thinking of quitting?" she asked hesitantly.

"I tried to quit, and they didn't want me to. This is their way of saying I can come back anytime I feel ready."

"You must be very valuable to them."

He shrugged. "I've been working for them for a long time. I'm one of the most experienced people they've got."

"You left on good terms, then?"

"Yeah. I loved that job. I love Africa. I'll miss . . . everything about the past fourteen years."

"Then why did you decide to leave?"

He stretched and let out a long breath. "I'm not exactly sure. I originally went there to hide from my life, and I —"

"What were you hiding from?" she interrupted.

"Oh, God, Gingie, everything." He rolled on his side and propped himself up on an elbow. Looking down at her, he said, "I grew up in the midst of publicity and scandal, and I just wanted total anonymity. I couldn't get that in the States, not with Jordan Hunter for a father and Adelina Marino for a mother. But nobody who lived in Morocco or Botswana or Zimbabwe cared who my parents were, and neither did the kind of Americans and Europeans who met me while I was guiding them around the bush in a truck."

He traced her dark eyebrows with one forefinger, his voice heavy with memory as he continued, "I didn't really care about seeing gorillas in the Virungas fourteen years ago. I just went on that trip as a confused twenty-year-old because I was trying to get away from it all, and that looked about as far away from my life as anything could be. Then one day, about two weeks into the trip, I realized that as far as the other dozen people camping with me were concerned, I was just Roe. Not Adehna Marino and Jordan Hunter's son, not Candy Jirrell's stepson, not a link in a famous chain. I was myself, alone, and I was judged only by my own virtues and faults. As far as I knew, that was the first time in my life that had happened to me."

"And it was what you needed," she murmured, kissing his fingertips as they brushed over her lips.

"In every way. I needed to be valued as myself, not as part of my crazy family. I needed a life-style of hard work and problems I could solve, instead of lots of money, lots of free time, and problems I could never solve."

"Your mother must have missed you."

He nodded. "She did. We had been very close, but from the day I first went to Africa until her death four years later, I only saw her three times. I was only able to call her about once every six weeks or so. She always sounded like such a typically Sicilian mother during those calls, too," he added wistfully. "'Are you eating enough? Are you well? Why don't you call more often? I pray to Santa Maria every night to save you from being eaten by a lion.'"

Gingie smiled. "Did you miss her?"

He was silent for a moment before answering, "Sometimes. But I was trying to get away from her, too. I knew by then that I couldn't prevent her from destroying herself, but hanging around while she was doing it had nearly killed me. I was a reckless, angry kid with no direction in those days, Gingie, and I indulged in every one of the addictions that my parents, my brother, and my sister have been grappling with all my life."

Hearing the pain in his voice, she took his hand and held it between her breasts. "But you've become so much more than that boy you're describing. You're purposeful and patient and strong, and you make people around you feel secure.

He kissed her and whispered, "I went through a lot of changes, Gingie. I quit the drugs, because I realized they were killing me. Then I quit the booze, because I saw what the stuff was doing to both of my parents, and I knew I could be next. I finally gave up cigarettes, too." He sighed. "I hardly even drink coffee anymore. With my family history, I figured I just couldn't afford to mess around."

"You went through more changes than that. You may have gone to Africa to hide from the world, but that's not all you've done there." He had grown into the man he was now.

"I was happy there. I just . . ." He shrugged. "I don't know, exactly. For the past couple of years I've felt like it's time to move on, to do something new. I'm thirty-four, and I've been living out of a backpack since I was twenty. I'm always either on the road or staying in company quarters. I have no home, except for this, and I don't want to live here full-time. I have no . . ." He paused before continuing, "I have no woman, no family of my own, no roots."

He lay on his back again, absently caressing her as he continued,

"When I realized that the feeling wasn't just a passing phase, I resigned. They offered me a permanent post in one of the operations centers, but I knew it was time to get out, to change my life. The thing is," he added, "I don't know what to do next. I went back to the States thinking that maybe it was time to go back for good. I guess I was thinking of starting my own business or buying some land. Something . . . solid."

"Are you tired of travelling?"

"No, I love to travel. I just want some stability."

"So, having been there, do you still think you'd like to settle in the States?" she asked.

"How could I?" he said bleakly. "Within three days, it was the same old scene."

"Your sister?" she whispered, seeing the pain in his face.

He sighed. "Yeah."

"What exactly happened, Roe?" He had resisted telling her so far, but she sensed that it was very important.

"I could see as soon as I got there that she'd been using again."

"Again? This was an old problem?"

He nodded. "She started even younger than I did. I went home for a few weeks when she was sixteen and saw it right away. Candy, of course, refused to believe it was anything to worry about, and my father was never around."

"What did you do?"

"I started to change my ways again."

"What do you mean?"

He stirred restlessly. "I survived my youth, in the end, by training myself not to interfere in other people's lives. It was hard to learn how, and I loved my mom so much that I had to go ten thousand miles away to save myself from going under with her."

She realized suddenly, and for the first time, how terribly guilty he still felt about that. Searching for wisdom, she said, "You had to, Roe. You and Vince, between the two of you, couldn't keep her from over-dosing, driving into canyons, passing out in the bathroom. You couldn't save her, and she couldn't nurture you, even though she was your mother. You had to get away. I'm sure she knew that, deep down."

He swallowed, staring at the ceiling. "The last time we talked on the phone, I was in the middle of another expedition. She asked me to come back home, to keep an eye on her for a while. Between the booze and the pills, she'd already missed two days of work on the new film, and they warned her . . ." He shook his head. "She wouldn't turn to Vince anymore, he was too domineering, but she needed someone. I begged her to go to AA, to quit the film, to go to a clinic, to come stay with me in Nairobi for a while. Anything. But I told her . . . I wouldn't police her anymore."

"So you refused to go back?" Gingie asked, aching for him.

He nodded. His chest started moving rapidly. "They found her dead two weeks later. I don't think she meant to overdose. I think she was just trying to stop the pain . . ." His voice cracked, and he squeezed his eyes shut. A moment later he whispered, "I've never told anyone else that she asked me to go back. You're the only one who knows, Gingie."

A hot tear slid down her cheek as she pressed her face against his heaving chest. She held him tightly, closing her eyes when he buried his face in her hair. "Thank you for telling me," she whispered. "You must know you couldn't have saved her, Roe."

"I don't know that, Gingie," he said heavily.

"But you —"

"Maybe I should have gone home and forced her to go into treatment. Maybe if I'd stepped in . . ."

"Maybe," Gingie said. "But she was in treatment before, and it didn't change anything for long. You couldn't make her *want* to get well, Roe." He stroked her back, silently thanking her for listening, for not judging him. At last, Gingie said, "So, the first time you realized Lisa was using, you thought it was time to step in?"

"Yes." He propped himself up against the pillows and admitted wearily, "But I didn't do anything very decisive the first time, or even when she was nineteen and I realized she was back on the stuff." He met Gingie's eyes. "I knew she got caught driving drunk last year, but I wasn't sure what I'd find when I went to LA this spring."

"What did you find?"

"She was sullen and high-strung, resentful of me for never being around, angry at our father, disgusted with her mother, insecure about her career, and obviously using again."

"Oh, Roe."

"Three days later, I found her nearly dead in her bedroom."

"She waited for you," Gingie said slowly, finally understanding. His eyes flashed up to her face, glittering gold. "She waited to do it until you were in LA with her. You were the only person she could count on to understand her cry for help. She knew you would take care of her."

"She still hasn't *forgiven* me for taking care of her," he said unhappily. When Gingie touched his cheek, where the scratches had already healed and faded away, he said, "She did that in the hospital when I told her she was going to a clinic. When she refused, I told her and Candy that if she didn't, I'd show her stash to the cops and turn her over to them, and *they* might not book her into such a nice place."

"Is she still mad?" Gingie asked, feeling his pain, wishing she could absorb it all for him. They all used him, and what did any of them give him in return except heartache? To Gingie, who had always received such love and nurturing from her family and friends, Roe's strength and resilience were extraordinary.

"I guess so," he answered. "She won't come to the phone whenever I call the clinic."

"She won't even talk to you?" Gingie was shocked. It was obviously too late to do anything about his mother, father, or stepmother, but she wanted to tell his sister how much he needed her. Even Roe couldn't give and give all the time without getting anything back.

"No." Seeing the utter despair in her expressive eyes, he smiled slightly, feeling warmed inside. "It's okay, Gingie."

It wasn't, and she knew it, but she simply held him fiercely and gave him all she could.

It was somewhere in the dark hours of that night, as she rested drowsily against his hard chest and listened to the deep, even sound of his breathing, that Gingie recognized what had already happened to her. And that was when she knew that she wanted them to live together, permanently, like her parents.

"I can give you what you need," she whispered, realizing with satisfaction how soundly he had slept ever since the night they had become lovers.

Ten

"Have you talked to Sandy yet?" Roe asked two days later.

Gingie shrugged as they roamed around the village with Milo and Zu Aspanu, selecting locations for the video. "It seems like I hardly see him lately," she said. "And every time I bring up the subject of his leaving, he refuses to talk about it."

"The phones are working again, so I have to call Vince this afternoon." Roe sounded resigned. "It will help the conversation along if I can tell him when Sandy's coming home. It's been two weeks since Vince started nagging us to send him back."

"I'll see what I can do," Gingie promised. Roe watched her with pleasure when she spotted a beautiful, crumbling courtyard, complete with flowering trees and a fountain, and bounded toward it with enthusiasm, dragging Milo behind her. Roe had never known anyone who took as much joy in life as Gingie.

And no one, he thought wryly, not even his mother, had ever questioned him so persistently. He was amazed, even embarrassed, at some of the things he had confided to her during the breezy, passion-scented nights that they lay wrapped together, drowsy with pleasure. How could he be expected to resist the sweet longing in her gaze, the affectionate curiosity in her honeyed voice, the alternately blunt and gentle way she phrased things? And he was surprised at how he had felt after telling her about his mother and Lisa — relieved to share the burden, grateful to Gingie for understanding, contented to be that much closer to her.

What am I going to do about you, Gingie?

He didn't know. How could he possibly go back to New York with her, after all? However he might feel about her, she was still Gingie; the eyes of the world were upon her and upon everyone around her. That life-style had killed his mother, turned his father into a paranoid, narcissistic lush, driven his sister to a nearly fatal overdose, and put his brother in the hospital with serious health problems.

"Roe! Come look at this!" Gingie cried, splashing Milo with water from the fountain. "Isn't it beautiful?"

How long could Gingie remain untouched by the excesses all around her? How long before she began crumbling, too? And seeing *that* would finally break him.

Gingie ran up to Roe to drag him into the courtyard with her. She stopped a moment later, frowning in concern. "What's wrong?"

Realizing how somber he must look as he gazed down at her with fear and regret twisting his heart, he shook his head and tried to smile. "I don't know. I'm a little tired, I guess." He realized that it was true. He felt sluggish and weary.

"Tired? I'm not surprised, after last night." She grinned deliciously and whispered, "You weren't kidding when you said you never do anything in moderation."

Remembering, he smiled more sincerely. "And I'm not just tired. I'm sore, too."

"*You're* sore?" she scoffed. "*I* have whisker burns between my thighs. Try living with that."

"It's not likely to become a problem in my life," he said dryly. Then he kissed her soft cheek and murmured in her ear, "But it might in yours."

She giggled and pushed his hand away when he caressed her bottom. A moment later, Milo beckoned them into the courtyard, smirking when he saw Gingie's flushed face.

"If you can concentrate on business for just a moment, Gin," Milo said, "I think this would be a good place for you to do the second verse of the song, don't you?"

Gingie nodded. "Yes, it's perfect, isn't it?"

"Yes, this place takes the cake," Zu Aspanu said. He wandered around the courtyard, contemplating the technical details.

"Roe," Milo said, "your uncle's a great guy, but have you ever noticed that he speaks in clichés?"

"What do you expect?" Roe said mildly. "He lived in Hollywood for a dozen years."

Milo considered this for a moment before joining Gingie in an exploration of the courtyard. Feeling kind of queasy for some reason, Roe plopped down quietly in the shade, insisting he was fine when Gingie remarked on how pale he suddenly looked. The last thing he needed was for her to decide he was ill and start pouring one of her noxious homeopathic potions down his throat.

With Milo's comments and suggestions, Gingie started marking out some of the basic blocking for the section of the video she wanted to film here. As soon as she started working, Roe noticed, her concentration was total and intensely focused. His mother had been like that. He had always admired that kind of artistic absorption, always been awed and mystified by it.

"When the bridge ends," Milo said, "you could step down . . ."

"And go over here," Gingie finished. She moved to the wall, her blond hair and funky clothes blending exotically with the blossoming flowers, creeping vines, and cracked stone. She sang a verse of her new song while Milo evaluated the scene and Zu Aspanu considered how to film it.

Gingie had already played the song for Roe, eager for his opinion, both insecure and arrogant about her creation, as gifted artists always were. The melody incorporated a hint of the minor-key exoticism of Sicily's ancient folk songs while the lyrics, mysterious and provocative, made him think of Sontara and Saint Cecilia.

The song, which she had decided to call *Untouched By Man*, reminded him, above all, of Gingie herself. She had honored him, giving herself to him after all the years of denying other men, and he was still awed by the wonder of her gift, by all the ways they found joy in each other now. He finally understood why he had never been able to resist her, not from the very first. Her astonishing magnetism was a by-product of the natural, pure beauty that bubbled out of her soul like heady champagne, too real to be disguised, too bountiful to be contained.

He had never known anyone like her, and he never would again. He enjoyed working with her, and he believed they created a balance that suited them both. He enjoyed caring for her, but he admired her enough to encourage her to keep spreading her wings. He felt a sense of belonging when he was with her, a diminishment of that rootless quality that had haunted him.

Yes, he wanted to stay with her, but he was afraid of watching her crumble, the way all the others had. When would Gingie start waking up with the shakes, being afraid to go out in public, living in constant terror of losing her gifts, giving in to the pressures surrounding her?

He shook his head and wiped sweat off his forehead, dizzy and grouchy, annoyed with the lump in his throat, chastising himself for growing pensive and maudlin on what should have been another pleasure-filled day. He forcibly shook off his gloom, taxing his strength as he did so.

As they left the courtyard, Milo said, "So Uncle Aspanu, have you ever seen *The Tempest?*"

"By Guilliermo Shakespeare?"

"That's the one," Milo confirmed. "There's this scene toward the end, before Prospero decides to return to the civilized world, where he finally shakes off these ghostly spirits that he's spent half the play messing with . . ."

Roe shook his head as Milo and the old man strolled ahead of him and Gingie. Subtlety was not Milo's strong point. Smiling at Gingie's abstracted expression, he took her hand to get her attention and said, "That's a beautiful song. It'll be one of your very best when it's recorded, Gingie."

"I identify with Saint Cecilia," she said simply. "She kept herself pure for her faith, and I kept myself pure for my art. We were both virgins when I began writing the song." She sighed pensively. "It's so sad, though. I met you, and I can still write and sing. She died alone and in pain. She must have been so brave."

Very much aware of Gingie's sensitivity and vulnerability in that moment, he raised her hand to his lips and kissed it tenderly, a private, intimate gesture. It made his blood run that much colder when he heard the sound of a camera shutter.

He looked up. The photographer wasn't alone. Two journalists had also spotted them and came tearing down the cobblestone street to speak to them.

"You're Prospero Hunter, aren't you?" a redheaded man asked.

Roe nodded, since denying it would be a waste of time.

Suddenly he, Gingie, and Milo were hit with a barrage of questions. Was there really going to be a video shot here on Sontara? Was it true that Sandy Stephen was involved? Was it true that Sandy Stephen was missing, as his manager said?

Had Roe and Gingie known each other long? Who was Milo seeing these days? Who was Gingie seeing these days? How long did Gingie plan to stay on Sontara?

Gingie handled the rapid-fire questions and photos with the ease of a seasoned performer. Plagued by dizziness and vague nausea, Roe tried to control his temper. He tried not to resent Gingie for this. He'd grown accustomed to the presence of her peculiar friends in his villa, to the speculations of the villagers, and to the scandalous stories Vince reported during every hysterical phone call, but *this* was too much. Especially with the way he felt right now, his stomach churning and his head pounding like the Doctor's drums.

He tried to stay calm and steer Gingie past these slick, aggressive people. His temper broke, however, when a dark-haired woman said in that too-familiar way, "Roe, how about a few comments on your sister's suicide attempt last month?"

Knowing it was the worst thing he could do, Roe snarled something utterly obscene at the woman, told the photographer where to stick his camera, and stormed away from the scene, ignoring the sound of Gingie's alarmed voice behind him.

"*I*'m sorry. I lost my temper, that's all," Roe said to Gingie when she came to his cottage that afternoon. It was the first time he'd seen her since stalking away that morning in the village.

"You don't seem like you've regained it," she said. "Whoofie says you were on the phone for nearly an hour when you got home, then you shut yourself in here as soon as I got back."

Stung by the innocent hurt in her voice, he snapped, "I needed a little time to myself, damn it! That's the reason I came to Sontara in the first place!"

After a heavy silence during which Roe endured worse guilt than he'd ever felt before, Gingie said, "Do you want to be alone? I can leave. I was just worried . . . I want to help you."

"Help me what?" he growled.

She didn't flinch. "I don't know. But something's wrong, and I can't just do nothing." She hesitated before adding, "You're upset because they asked about your sister, aren't you?"

"Celebrities have no secrets, do they?" he said bitterly.

"Of course, they do. *I* do."

"No, you don't. What do you want to bet that every scandalmonger in America knows by now that we're lovers?"

"You're wrong," she said quietly. "They don't know. It doesn't matter what they say or print, they don't know the truth. They've written that I'm lovers with Sandy, with Milo, with Vince, with Luke Swain, with a French film star whose name I can't remember." She shrugged. "It doesn't matter. It would only matter if I cared what they thought, and I don't. I don't need to."

Exhausted and undeniably cranky, he said, "We have to talk."

"Okay, but you should sit down. You don't look good, Roe."

He felt like arguing, just for the satisfaction of snapping at someone, but she was right. He needed to sit down. He sat on the love seat, keeping his distance from her. Confusion and pain tore at his belly. He wanted to hold her, to burrow into her for comfort, but he also wanted to lash out at her for breaking him into little pieces this way. Why, of all the women he'd ever known, did it have to be Gingie that he couldn't even fall asleep without anymore?

"I had a long talk with Vince today," he began.

"Is he better?" she asked quickly.

Roe nodded. "Despite a few complications, mostly brought about by his bouts of hysteria, he's doing well. But his doctors are very definite about what he has to do if he wants to live to a ripe old age."

"What's that?"

"He has to find a quieter line of work."

"You mean . . ." She paused, thinking it through. "He can't be my manager anymore?"

"No, Gingie. So you've got to find a new one right away. Vince says he has a couple of people in mind, but I've convinced him that the final decision should be yours. You've got to go back to New York to settle this. I can book you a flight —"

"No!" Trying to calm down, she added, "I don't want to leave you."

Her simple statement caused pain in his heart as well as his belly. "According to Vince, this won't wait. You've got to go."

"Then come with me," she urged.

"What?"

"Or call Vince and tell him I . . ." Her eyes widened. "Tell him I want to hire you."

"Are you nuts?"

"No, it's perfect!" she insisted eagerly, scooting closer to him. "Don't you see? We work so well together, and you said you wanted something new."

"I said I wanted stability," he corrected. "Managing a rock group is hardly —"

"You'll have stability, too. You'll have me. I'm stable. And I'll have you, which is what I've always needed."

"And we'll both have a lot of problems," he said irritably.

"Don't say that." She held his gaze, her own shimmering with strange blue lights. "Roe, I love you. We should be together."

His mind was spinning, and her lovely face was going in and out of focus. "Are you kidding? How long before I scoop you off the bathroom floor, too, and send you to a drug clinic?"

"What?" She blinked at him, confused by his garbled, low-pitched question. He looked dreadfully pale and he was sweating.

"How many photographers will live outside our front door? How long before we . . . we . . ."

"Roe?" Gingie took his hand and touched his perspiring face. "You're burning up! And your pulse is like a rabbit's!"

"Oh, God . . ." He should have known. If he hadn't been so distracted, he would have recognized the signs — fatigue, queasiness, depression, irritability, dizziness. "It's the malaria," he mumbled. "I'm sorry, Gingie."

"Malaria!"

He wanted to laugh at the way she practically shrieked in his ear, but he was just too tired. "It's okay, don't worry. I've had it before."

"We've got to get you to a doctor!"

"No, just help me get to bed," he ordered, his voice slurred. "And *don't* get a doctor. I don't need him, and even if I did . . ."

"Roe, you can't just —"

"The only doctor on Sontara is Don Ciccio's nephew, and everyone knows he bribed his way through med school."

"What should I do?" she asked desperately, helping him to the bed, alarmed by how heavily he needed to lean upon her, by how hot and flushed his skin was. No doctor? "How can I help you?"

"Help me get my clothes off, then get me some water."

With that done, she asked, "What else?"

"I'll be okay," he said groggily. "Just leave me alone to sweat it out."

"No! Roe, you look ready to die!"

He smiled vaguely as she pushed him back into the pillows and pulled the sheet over his naked body. "I'm used to it, Gingie. It wasn't even so bad after the first seven or eight times."

"This happens to you often?" she asked in horror.

He closed his eyes and pulled the sheet up to his chin. "About once a year." He shivered slightly and added, "Maybe not that often. Doesn't last much more than a day anymore."

"Well, I'm not leaving you alone, Roe. We're not even going to discuss that. You might as well tell me how to help you."

"My Florence Nightingale," he murmured weakly.

She took his clammy hand between hers. "I love you."

"That's what hurts so much," he mumbled. "I love you, too."

In that case, Gingie decided, he was coming back to New York with her whether he wanted to or not. And her first priority, she reasoned, was helping him get well enough to discuss it. Within minutes of getting into bed, he fell into a stupor, mumbling a little bit, moving fitfully, but not really conscious at all.

After about an hour of this, Gingie called Milo to sit with him so she could phone her sister in New York. Then, informed about how to care for Roe until Letitia's arrival, she returned to his side, assuring Milo that she knew exactly what she was doing.

Roe's fever rose all evening, and his skin was burning hot by night fall. That was when he became delirious. Although Letitia had warned Gingie about this, it nonetheless terrified her at first. She could scarcely understand anything he said during the long hours that he tossed and turned, shivering with cold and burning with fever, clinging to her hands as he mumbled and cried out. Sometimes she could recognize a name — his mother, his brother, his sister, people she'd never heard of — but his speech was mostly repetitive, garbled nonsense, fueled by fear, sadness, and anger. It was a shame, she thought, that no one ever seemed to relive their *happiest* moments when they were delirious.

She cared for him as best she could, following all of Letitia's instructions, hoping that she didn't mix them up. Letitia had warned her to remain cool-headed, but how could she, when Roe was in such torment?

It wasn't until early morning that he became even slightly lucid. Shivering, his skin still flushed and hot, he called her name. Damp with sweat and stiff with fatigue, Gingie whispered, "I'm here. It's all right. I'm right here."

"Cold," he muttered. Then he added, "Don't leave me."

"I won't," she murmured, stroking his sweat-soaked hair. "I love you." She tried to give him one of Letitia's herbal infusions then, but he spit it out with a very obscene comment.

Hours later, when her back ached from bending over him again and again and her eyes were raw from lack of sleep, she finally realized he was resting comfortably. She curled up in the hard wooden chair she had dragged over to the bed and studied his face — the dark skin, the high cheekbones, the strong jaw, the straight nose. He looked handsome even now. She smiled, thinking about how he would shrug dismissively when she told him.

"Gingie," Milo chided, entering the cottage a little while later. "You haven't touched any of the food I've brought you."

"I'm not hungry," she answered tiredly.

"It must be love."

"It is," she said with quiet sincerity.

Milo come to stand by the bed. "Does he know?"

"Yes, but he didn't seem to take it very well." She sighed. "I managed to pick a man who's spent his entire adult life trying to get away from famous people."

"Hasn't had much luck, has he? You can never escape your destiny," Milo said philosophically. "Look at me."

"I think he's afraid he'll wind up right back where he started," she said pensively. "But I'm not at all like the rest of his family."

"He'll figure it out," Milo assured her. "He's a bright boy. Besides, he's hopelessly in love. He's fighting it, of course, but any halfwit can see that he's hooked. Just reel him in, Gingie."

"I'll have to wait till he wakes up."

"Don Ciccio called a little while ago. He's driving Letitia out right now. Why don't you go inside and wait for her? I'll sit with Roe for a while."

"No, I —"

"Go on," Milo ordered. "You're the one who sent for her."

After casting a longing look at Roe, Gingie said, "Maybe you're right. I have to make a few calls, anyhow."

*H*is head pounding and his muscles stiff, Roe stirred groggily and opened his eyes. "What are you doing here?" he asked Milo, who sat on a chair by the bed, reading a copy of a music magazine.

"You're alive!" said Milo. "I thought this was a wake."

Roe groaned. "Not yet. How long have I been out?"

Milo glanced at his watch. "About twenty-six hours."

"Not so bad. It used to last two or three days."

"What a tough guy," Milo drawled.

"Oh, I'm sure I whined a lot during the night."

"I wouldn't know. Gingie was with you, not me."

"She was here?" Roe frowned, then, remembering, he nodded. "Yeah, she was here."

"All night. Wouldn't even eat. That's pretty serious, Roe."

"I told her not to stay," Roe muttered.

"You didn't really think she'd listen, did you?" When Roe scowled and looked away, Milo leaned forward and said, "She's a pretty high-maintenance chick, it's true, but you seem to have overlooked the most important point. Gingie likes to take care of other people even more than she needs to be taken care of herself. She's let me live with her for a year, and she's been baby-sitting Sandy ever since he got to New York. Roe, you could have an attack like this every week, instead of every year, and she'd still stay up all night with you. God help the silly woman, she loves you."

"Milo, I —"

"I know what you're thinking, man. You come from a pretty grim background, the Hollywood fairy tale turned into a nightmare. To live the way we do, it's true that everyone needs a crutch. Unfortunately, your relatives keep choosing crutches that can kill them. But not everybody does, Roe." Milo took off his glasses and looked at them consideringly. "Personally, I find that looking at the world through rose-tinted lenses helps me. You may not believe this, but I used to be a pretty cynical fellow."

"I'd never have guessed."

Milo added, "This also gives me a bit of privacy, since no one can see my eyes."

"I've noticed," Roe muttered.

Putting his glasses back on, Milo continued, "Gingie's method is much more simple, and probably more durable. She's just oblivious. Haven't you noticed? I've been with her for twelve years, and I've never seen it get to her. Not once." Milo shrugged. "Now, you can figure that that's a pretty good track record and she'll probably keep it up. Or you can go back to the bush and be lonely the rest of your life. Think it over, Roe."

And with that, Milo got up and left the cottage. While he considered that rather extraordinary speech, Roe eased himself out of bed, grimacing when his tired, aching muscles protested. He had no patience with his weakness. There was too much to do right now, too much to think about. He padded barefoot and naked into the bathroom and turned on the shower spray, soothing his body and refreshing his mind with the hot steam of water.

Based on what he could remember about yesterday, he figured Gingie had put up with a hell of a lot. After his display of temper, not to mention the hurt that his gnawing indecision and harsh rejection must have caused her, he thought he owed it to her to sort out his thoughts before she came bounding back into his cottage.

There were no guarantees, and there never had been. He didn't mind that life was hard and unpredictable. He only knew that he couldn't watch someone else he loved destroy herself, consumed by public demand and the weight of her own talent.

But, feeling clearheaded at last, he also recognized that Milo was right. His fears had made him foolish, clouding his mind. Gingie was, as he himself had once said, a woman of enormous personal resources. And that strange, quixotic, untouchable quality that made her what she was, would, he had to believe, protect her from the fate Roe had seen too many times.

He had been a caretaker for too long. Now he and Gingie could take care of each other, he realized. He would shelter her, as he yearned to, but he would finally be sheltered in return. She had proved that in so many ways, in the open heart she offered him when they made love, in the silent sympathy of her listening, in the persistent questions she showered upon him when he was moody, in her resilient reaction to his temper, in the way she appeased his fears and nurtured him in his illness.

Feeling shaky about the next step, but knowing there was no turning back, he stepped out of the shower and began toweling himself off. He was slipping into his robe when he heard the door to the cottage open.

He came out of the bathroom, belting the robe around his waist, as nervous about talking to Gingie as if he were one of her fans.

Her lovely blue eyes sparkled when she saw him. "Milo said you were awake!" she said joyfully. "But should you be up?"

"I needed a shower. I felt like the inside of an old shoe."

She smiled, her blood warming to the sandpaper quality of his voice. She was carrying a tray of Letitia's special preparations and, feeling it grow heavy, she set it down on the table. "I'm glad you look more like yourself. You scared me."

"You look awful," he said frankly. Her eyes were red, her hair was messy, and her face was drawn. But her radiant smile warmed him, and, paradoxically, she had never looked lovelier.

"Well, I was up all night with you. I can't be expected to be glamorous all of the time, Roe. You'll have to get used to that."

"Gingie, we have to talk."

"Yes, we do. But first, Letitia says you should drink all of this, and eat that."

"You called her?" he asked weakly, stalling.

"She's here."

"Here?"

"When you got sick last night, I called her in New York and told her to come right away, in case you didn't get well as fast as you said you would." Seeing his expression, she added, "Well, I obviously couldn't call the local doctor, after what you said."

"No, I guess not," he conceded. He took a sip from the mug she pressed into his hands, then screwed up his face. "I don't —"

"All of it," she ordered, her voice unusually stern.

"All of it?" he repeated bleakly. When she nodded, he took her hand and drew her over to the bed, where they sat together. "Gingie, we —"

"Oh, I called Vince a little while ago. He's pacified for the moment. Sandy will be leaving for New York tomorrow morning." She smiled and added, "And Maria Sellerio and her grandmother will be going to visit him next week. I think he plans to marry her."

Roe choked on his infusion. "What? How did that happen?"

Gingie shrugged. "Kindred spirits, I guess. As far as I know, Maria is the first woman besides me that Sandy has spoken to voluntarily in over a year. The funny thing is, she speaks no more English than he speaks Italian."

"Language of the heart, I guess," Roe said dryly.

"That's why we've hardly seen him around lately, and why he wouldn't leave Sontara. He was courting Maria."

"And now he's going to have Signor Sellerio's cranky old mother-in-law chaperoning him in New York. It's some life you rock stars lead."

"I'm happy for him," Gingie said.

"So am I," Roe admitted. "She'll give him some stability. And . . ." He traced the back of Gingie's pale hand with his forefinger. "I guess this will free you up for a new escort."

"I don't want any more escorts." She met his gaze. "Or baby-sitters."

"I . . . know."

"I want you," she said steadily. "I need you."

His voice shook as he answered, "I need you, too."

She grasped his hand. "Then stay with me. For good."

"Stepping into your way of life scares me, Gingie," he admitted quietly.

"I know." She licked her lips, aware of how much was at stake here. "But I wouldn't have spent my whole life climbing to the top, Roe, if I were the kind of person who could give it up." She paused. "I can't pretend there'll be any peace and quiet, and there certainly won't be any anonymity."

"I don't —"

"There's only me," she interrupted, wanting to finish. "And I love you." Her eyes misted. "I love you so much, Roe. Nobody else understands me so well, or makes me feel so good."

His heart filling with a wonderful, extraordinary ache, he took her in his arms and held her, his face pressed into the scented hollow of her neck. "I love you," he murmured. "Let's take care of each other." He smiled ruefully a moment later, "If you can handle my moods and my malaria and my relatives, I suppose I can handle the scandalmongers."

"Really?" she whispered, squeezing her eyes shut as she pressed her face into his shoulder and inhaled deeply. "Then . . . you'll come live with me in New York?"

"Yeah, but I don't want to live with Milo and Letitia, too. Let's get our *own* place." He stroked her hair. He had expected this step to terrify him, but he felt relieved and elated, instead. "And I'll tell Vince that I'll be taking over for him."

"You will?" She laughed delightedly and gave him a quick, enthusiastic kiss. "Oh, Roe!"

"But things are going to be different," he warned her. "You're going to do more for yourself. For one thing, you're going to get a checkbook." She nodded, and he added, "And we won't need to worry about your volatile relationship with record companies anymore, either."

"Why not?"

"I'm going to start my own label — Sontara."

"Really?" Gingie was wide-eyed.

"It'll take some time. I don't know anything about it, but I'll learn. I didn't know anything about surviving in the bush fourteen years ago, but I became the best expedition guide in the company. Anyhow, Gingie, I can't just spend my time being Mr. Virginia Potter. I need something of my own. I know that much about myself."

Smiling tenderly, Gingie said, "You're right." She snuggled happily in his arms and asked, "We don't have to leave here as soon as the video's done, do we?"

He brought her hand to his lips and kissed it. "No. I want to stay awhile. Maybe, just maybe, we can get all of these people out of the house and have some peace and quiet together." When he saw the way Gingie's eyes shifted, he asked suspiciously, "What is it?"

"Well, when Letitia called my parents to tell them how beautiful it is here, they naturally expressed interest. And I . . ." She shrugged. "I'm afraid I invited them, Roe. Well, they are my parents. And then I talked to Camilla, and I naturally . . ."

"Oh, Gingie," he said wearily.

"There's another boat out in the bay, too," she continued. "They seem to have TV cameras with them this time. And you might have a little trouble in the village, since the pharmacist apparently blabbed to Signora Gambarossa about —"

"I'll kill him," Roe exclaimed. Then he sighed and said, "Never mind. We can put a stop to the gossip by getting married right away. All right?"

"Oh, no. We can't get married, Roe," Gingie said earnestly.

His world suddenly bottoming out, he demanded, "Why not? What happened to love and stability and —"

"Well, we can have all that, Roe. It's just that the members of my family don't approve of marriage. It would cause so much trouble if we did it."

"They don't approve of marriage?" he repeated incredulously. "But what about your parents? Surely they —"

"Oh, they're not married," Gingie said. "My mother says that marriage represents women as chattel, that it imprisons them in the role of property, which —"

"I get the picture." After giving her an exasperated look, he said, "But I come from an old Sicilian family of very strict beliefs, so we're just going to have to do it, Gingie. I'm sure I can explain it to your mother."

"If you say so, Roe." She ran her hands down her hips. "I wonder what I should wear?"

"I'm sure you'll think of something," he said dryly, wondering what Gingie's version of a wedding gown was going to look like.

"Oh, and that's not all."

"What else?" he asked patiently.

"Your sister is coming for a visit as soon as she's released from the clinic."

He went absolutely still. "Lisa?"

"Yes. We had a nice long chat this afternoon. She's a little confused, but I like her, Roe."

"She *talked* to you?"

"Oh, yes. She's going to teach me to sail when she gets here." Gingie traced her fingers across his lean cheek. "She loves you very much, you know. She just didn't realize how much you needed her."

"And you . . . made her see the light," Roe said, as amazed as ever by this woman who had chosen to love him. "My secret weapon," he murmured. "I should have turned you loose on her weeks ago."

She kissed him tenderly. "So it might be a while before we get that peace and quiet you were talking about."

"A while? Who am I kidding? It's liable to be thirty or forty years." He felt more cheerful about that than he would have thought possible.

"You don't mind?" she asked tentatively.

"Let's say I'm willing to compromise," he amended.

"You *said* you wanted roots and family," she reminded him.

"I was thinking along the lines of children, Gingie, not an endless supply of in-laws."

"You love children, don't you?" Gingie asked, thinking of the way all the children on Sontara adored him, of the way he had cared for his little sister for so many years.

"I love children," he agreed. "But I've always been afraid —"

"You'll make a wonderful father," she assured him. Her heart swelling with love, her eyes flashing over the muscular chest revealed by the V-neck of his bathrobe, and her body warming to the alluring heat of his skin, she whispered, "Let's make a baby together."

"Now?" His lashes lowered over eyes that were glittering with exotic gold highlights. A flush stole across his strong cheekbones, and he shifted slightly as his body reacted to her touch.

Smiling, she pressed him back into the pillows. "You're still weak. I'll be gentle." She kissed him fleetingly, several times.

"You're a tease," he told her a moment later.

"That's not teasing," she chided, slowly parting his robe down the length of his hard body. Her gaze drifted down and then, with a slow, seductive smile, she lowered her head, murmuring, *"This* is teasing you." Her mouth closed over him, hot and tender.

He groaned and let his head fall back against the soft pillow, his breath gusting harshly in and out of his lungs as she tormented him.

"Is this how you told me you like it?" she asked innocently.

"I . . . Ohh, yeah." Then, he suddenly gasped in surprise and added in a strangled vice, "But I never even thought of *that."* A moment later he arched off the bed as she tried something else he was sure he'd never taught her. Her songs, he realized, should have warned him what a fertile imagination she had.

"Do you like that?" she whispered.

He clutched the side of the mattress, panting wildly as he tried to control his spiraling excitement. "You've got to be kidding," he croaked. "Gingie, stop. I'm going to . . . to . . ."

Smiling, she laid her cheek against his flat stomach and watched his face as he struggled with his arousal. He apparently gave up a moment later, for his hands seized her shoulders and he drew her roughly against him. His kiss was deep and drugging, his tongue probing and insistent, his hands greedy and restless. "I thought of that last night," she admitted breathlessly, closing her eyes rapturously as his lips explored the hollow between her breasts. "I felt kind of guilty, actually. You were delirious, and I was sponging down your naked body and thinking about sex."

"It's okay," he assured her, his lips moving urgently over her face and neck. "It was *worth* being delirious." He kissed her again. "You never cease to amaze me."

"I can do it again," she offered, thrilled by her newfound power.

His tortured puff of laughter brushed her hair. "Not just now, Gingie. I'm going to explode any minute."

He rose above her and started pulling off her clothes. "So much for being ill and weak," she murmured.

"So much for being masterful," he said a moment later, getting confounded by the combination of stockings, leggings, and shorts she was wearing, as well as by the series of jangling chains that apparently held them all up. "Take off your clothes."

She stripped slowly for him, making him ache even more, making him think how desperately twenty million men in America would envy him at this moment. Eager to bury himself inside her, yearning to make her moan with pleasure, he pulled her beneath him while she was still half-dressed. Her arms slid around him, her palms stroking his back as her legs parted for him. He explored her gently with his hand, making sure she was ready for him, then he slid into her hot, snug, welcoming femininity, groaning with pleasure as he sank home inside her.

Gingie's hands touched him greedily, reveling in the bunch and flow of his shoulder muscles as he thrust into her again and again, creating the sweetest music she'd ever known. His taut, hard buttocks flexed rhythmically under her palms as he pushed his knees against the mattress and pulled her hips higher, whispering erotically to her as his hot mouth teased her tender nipples.

He watched her as she climaxed, and she showed him openly and uninhibitedly how much pleasure he gave her, how much love spilled through her veins when he poured himself inside her. She stroked his silky hair as he shuddered and sank weakly down upon her, gracefully giving himself up to her body's embrace. Eyes closed, she rested her cheek against his hair and, when she could move, stretched out her long legs so they wouldn't cramp. He rested in her arms, as weak as a kitten, giving her his vulnerability, trusting her to treasure this special gift.

"I love you," he murmured at last, his voice rich with satisfaction.

"There's nothing like this," she sighed.

"Nothing," he agreed.

"But it's a little like giving a concert," she added.

"Really?" He rolled lazily away and looked at her curiously.

"Well," she said, touching him, marveling at his masculine beauty, "every time I do it, I'm more confident that I know what I'm doing, and I remember how good it was the time before, so I'm more excited. And, somehow, it just gets better every time."

He kissed her softly. "I see what you mean." He pulled her to rest against his chest and added, "But, unlike a concert, we don't have thousands of people watching us when we do this."

She laughed at the thought. Then she slid her arm around him and said pensively, "That makes this even more special. This is our secret. No one in the world knows what we do when we're alone together."

"I think they can make a pretty good guess," he said dryly.

"They know we make love, but that's all they know. In this respect, my life is as private as anyone else's," she said with satisfaction. "They don't know *how* we make love, what we say to each other, how we make each other feel, or what we talk about afterward. This is ours alone."

He realized she was right, and that there were many other things between them that would always remain private. It was enough. Feeling grateful to her for her strength and wisdom, he squeezed her shoulder. A moment later he asked, "Do you really want a baby right now?"

"If you've given me one already, I want it," she said with certainty. "If not . . ."

"Yes?"

"I was thinking, maybe after we settle into New York and after I finish my summer tour, we could go on another vacation together. I've never been to Africa."

"You want to go?" he asked, trying to keep his voice neutral. The thought of Gingie running loose in the remote wilds of the Okavango Delta, bartering freely with the merchants of Morocco, tracking game with a camera in Zimbabwe, preaching her family's feminist principles to the women of Kenya . . . Roe thought he felt a headache coming on.

"Oh, yes, Roe," she said enthusiastically, pleased that he hadn't simply rejected the idea. "You've made me realize how much I've missed. I've done two world tours without seeing anything except hotel rooms and concert stadiums."

"Maybe we should think small at first," he said carefully.

"I could probably get away for a month or two, don't you think?" she rushed on, getting excited. "Milo will be thrilled, too. He's always wanted to see the pyramids. He's pretty adamant about not climbing to the top, though," she added.

Roe tried to picture Milo, who thought it was cruel and unusual punishment to be separated from his microwave, going on safari with them. "Maybe Milo won't —"

"And I can learn how to cook over a campfire. Won't it be wonderful?"

Shifting so that her long, silky body rested more comfortably against him, he tried to picture it. "All I can see," he said at last, "is me having to rescue a dozen tabloid photographers from being trampled by hippos, getting attacked by predators, or drowning in the Nile as they follow us around the continent trying to get a scoop on you."

"Oh, you don't have to save them, Roe," Gingie assured him. "They can fend for themselves. Anyhow, it's not as if they were *invited.*"

"What the hell," Roe said, his sense of humor winning out at last. "Let's do it."

"Really?" she asked eagerly.

"Sure. I'm ready for anything."

"Oh, Roe!" She sprawled across him and covered his face with kisses. "We'll have such a good time!"

"I know," he sighed. "That's what makes it worth the effort."

About the Author

*L*aura Leone is the award-winning author of more than a dozen romance novels, two of which are set in Sicily, where she was living when she decided to write her first book. Under her real name, Laura Resnick, she is also the Campbell Award-winning author of more than thirty science fiction/fantasy short stories, as well as several epic fantasy novels. In addition, she is the author of *A Blonde In Africa,* a non-fiction account of the eight months she spent traveling across Africa (several years after writing *The Black Sheep).* You can can find her on the Web at: http://www.sff.net/people/laresnick.

Printed in the United States
22329LVS00005B/433

9 781587 151880